DEATH ON DISPLAY

A CHARLETON HOUSE MYSTERY

KATE P ADAMS

Copyright © Kate P Adams 2023

The right of Kate P Adams to be identified as the author of this work has been asserted by her in accordance with the Copyright, Designs and Patents Act 1988.

All rights reserved. No part of this publication may be reproduced, transmitted, or stored in a retrieval system, in any form or by any means, without permission in writing from the author, nor be otherwise circulated in any form of binding or cover other than that in which it is published and without similar condition being imposed on the subsequent purchaser.

All characters in this publication, other than those clearly in the public domain, are fictitious and any resemblance to real people, alive or dead, is purely coincidental.

Cover design by Dar Albert

ALSO BY KATE P ADAMS

THE CHARLETON HOUSE MYSTERIES

Death by Dark Roast

A Killer Wedding

Sleep Like the Dead

A Deadly Ride

Mulled Wine and Murder

A Tragic Act

A Capital Crime

Tales from Charleton House

Well Dressed to Die

Death on Display

THE JOYCE AND GINGER MYSTERIES

Murder En Suite

Murder in the Wings

*In memory of my mum,
who shared my love of crime fiction.*

1

The fleas were dressed as circus performers, balancing on tightropes, juggling, or riding bicycles. Two were wearing their wedding finery, one in a dinner jacket, the other in a white lace dress. One flea had been kitted out as a cowboy and was chasing another that had been made to look like a horse on the run. Quite apart from the need for excellent eyesight and the patience of a saint, I really couldn't understand what would drive someone to spend presumably days, if not weeks and months, making such a bizarre display. It had been created in 1905 when there was no TV or internet, but still, it took an unusual mind to even think of it.

'That's nothing,' called Mark from across the gallery. 'Take a look at this.'

I pulled my attention away from a particularly talented flea that was throwing knives at one of its fellow Siphonaptera and had so far missed with every throw, and joined my overexcited friend.

'Look, over here, these are incredible.' Mark was examining the contents of specimen jars which contained an array of animals in various stages of life and death, or they had been when they were pickled. He looked right at home amongst the museum display cases in his tie and waistcoat, a colourful handkerchief poking out from his top pocket. The neatly curled handlebar moustache nicely completed the picture of an eccentric collector.

'I'm glad I ate before we came here.' I really did feel queasy. I had come to the Pilston many times in my formative years – it was the museum that every local child had visited on a school trip at least once by the time they were ten, and I'd been more times than I could count, but not for more than twenty years. The fleas had fascinated me as a youngster, but the jars I didn't recall. It could be my increasingly bad memory, or my teachers and parents might have steered me away from them. It was also possible that some of the collection had been swapped out over the years.

Everything about the Victorian museum brought memories flooding back. The dusty, musty smell, the shadowy galleries, the eyes of the stuffed animals staring out at me, the little booklets we answered questions in as we went around, and the stories we had to write about our visit once we got back to school. I recalled my excitement at going into the gift shop to buy the obligatory pencil and eraser, then counting out the change to see if I could afford any of the sweets that were displayed on the counter. I remembered a friend giving me two pence so I could have a little bag of pear drops, my favourites back in the day.

Mark disturbed my reminiscing. 'Alright, come on, we'll play it safe. I won't make you stare at the incredible wonders of nature,' he said, sounding like a comically exaggerated parent. He was peering at a frog with a particularly hideous-looking way of spawning its young. Mark screwed up his face and stepped back. 'Which even I have to admit look like props from a horror film at times.' He led me across a mezzanine which looked down onto a hall filled with more wood and glass cases, and I wondered who did the cleaning, because the tops of the cases were covered in a layer of dust. As we walked down a flight of stairs, he continued to tell me the history of this small local museum, which I could remember little about.

'The current Lord Eyre's great-grandfather created the museum as a way of housing his ever-growing collection of natural curiosities, and then opened it to the public in 1890. He was a great traveller and, as was the way in those days, he was always returning from exotic locations with trunks full of beautiful but dead specimens, the odder the better, which he then went on to have stuffed – not always accurately – and put on display.'

'Odd is an understatement,' I said, thinking about the flea on the tightrope.

'Yeah, the family have always had an unusual streak in them, although the current Lord Eyre is a very nice chap and as down to earth as they come. I had tea with him yesterday.'

'Did you indeed? I hope you kept your pinkie in the air.'

'As the actress said to the bishop,' he responded. I let that one slide, I deserved it. Both Mark and I worked for the Duke and Duchess of Ravensbury, members of one of the higher-ranking aristocratic families in the country, so teasing him about having tea with a lord was a wasted gag. And as he had reminded me on numerous occasions, the upper classes do not stick their little finger out. Only those who aspire to fit in with them do that.

'Ananya and I are still finalising what will go on display, but we're almost done. Lord Eyre and the Duke will then have final approval. They've let us have quite a lot of free rein, but it's their ancestors after all. Only they'd better be quick, we have three days to get this all finished and on display.'

Mark Boxer, who works at Charleton House, where I run the cafés, and Ananya Shah from Berwick Hall – home of the Eyre family – had been given an unusual and impressive opportunity for a couple of tour guides. They were curating a small exhibition about the partnership of Edward 'Teddy' Fitzwilliam-Scott, the great-grandfather of our employer the twelfth Duke of Ravensbury, and Lord Decimus Eyre, the current lord's grandfather. By far the younger of the two, Decimus had travelled the world, as his father had done. Teddy, a party-loving socialite, threw money at the expeditions, and then basked in the associated glory of discovery, but had no interest in going himself. Besides which, he was getting on in years and was happy to let the youngster take the risk of death and disease on some of the more perilous journeys.

'I thought that concentrating quite so much on the dig in Egypt was a bit old hat. Everyone has a sarcophagus on display and photographs of white men in pith helmets peering into recently dug holes, surrounded by awestruck locals, but apparently it's what the current lord wants, and who am I to argue? Also, the chair of the trustees is a bit of an Egyptian history nut and has been obsessed with some of the collection here since he was a child. It's hardly Lord Carnarvon at Highclere, but there are some beautiful objects.'

It was Lord Carnarvon who had discovered the tomb of Tutankhamun in 1922 and there was a superb exhibition all about the dig at his home, Highclere Castle, which had gained more recent fame after appearing in *Downton Abbey* on TV.

'Old hat? How dare you!' We turned to face a smiling man. 'Mark, you shall be lashed with a stick 100 times, and then thrown in the river with crocodiles.'

'So long as it's a historically accurate punishment, I'm fine with it. Good morning, Sheridan.'

'I'll add another fifty lashes if you don't start calling me Shed.'

'Apologies. Shed, meet my friend Sophie. Sophie works with me at Charleton House. Sophie, this is Sheridan... sorry, *Shed* Tasker, chair of the trustees.'

'Lovely to meet you, Sophie. Receiving a behind-the-scenes tour?' Shed looked to be in his sixties, a well-lined face framing a broad smile. 'Mark is right, I've long been fascinated with Egyptian history. I would come here as a child and spend hours just staring at the collection, and then badgering any staff member who was unfortunate enough to come by with questions.'

'Do you work in the field now?' He would make a wonderful teacher, enthusing students with his passion.

'No, no. Have you heard of Tasker biscuits?' I had. I was known to gorge on their butter crunch with its thin line of jam running through the middle, or their chocolate pecan delights which had the perfect amount of chocolate and nut lumps. 'Well, that's me, or it was until I sold the business. Now I get to indulge my own personal whims. Which reminds me, Mark, Lord Eyre has had permission from his brother to borrow the Bastet statue for the exhibition. You should see it, Sophie, it's a particularly good example of a statuette of the Goddess Bastet, who was typically pictured as a cat-headed woman or in the form of a cat. Apparently, the brother doesn't like to let it out of his sight, so this is a bit of a coup.'

'If you'd said you wanted cats, I can think of a particularly queen-like specimen who would look good stuffed and in a glass case, where she can't cause any trouble.'

Shed looked confused. I glared at Mark.

'I do apologise, Shed. My friend, and I use the word advisedly, is referring to my own cat, Pumpkin, who Mark has a very unreasonable and unjustified dislike of.'

'I described her as queen like, and she would be on display to illustrate how the Egyptians viewed cats as divine symbols. It would be an honour for her, and I could save the museum money by stuffing her myself. A few bags of cotton wool balls, a week in the freezer to get rid of any mites and we'd be good to go.'

Shed laughed. 'Are you sure you two aren't married?'

2

'Married to you? Can you imagine? I will never live that suggestion down,' said Mark, with feigned horror. Or at least, I hoped he was feigning.

'Serves you right for talking about putting Pumpkin on display.'

'I told you, it's a sign of respect. She would have been worshipped back then.'

'Well, she's worshipped right now, by me.' I thought about that for a minute. It sounded odd. Pumpkin was an overweight distributor of cat hair who demanded food, water and the most comfortable spots in the house, and all in return for zero rent or work. I rarely got a night of undisturbed sleep thanks to her antics, and I'd stepped in cat vomit more times than I cared to remember. But despite all that, there was nothing better than being woken by the loud purring of my fat, furry tabby.

Mark and I had left the galleries, with their atmospheric collection of antique wood and glass display cases, and entered a rabbit warren of white plaster corridors, which all looked a bit the worse for wear and in desperate need of a lick of paint.

'I'll show you what I've been working on.' Mark led me into a basement room. Before us a large sarcophagus, resting on a wooden pallet, was being carefully dusted by a man who was using what looked to me like an artist's paintbrush. He had earphones on, and I could hear the tinny sound of his music. He didn't bother to look up.

Although now dulled in colour and with chips of paint missing here and there, the sarcophagus was still an impressive object. The eyes stared straight ahead, capped by blue eyebrows, and blue and red stripes framed its face. What had once been shimmering gold formed a crisscross pattern over the body, hieroglyphics telling stories on all available space.

'Imagine ending up on display, thousands of eyes peering at you,' I said, taking in the beautiful detail.

'We're not putting him on display, it's empty.'

'Where is he, whoever *he* was?'

'He was Masahanum and he's gone for treatment and analysis. A spa for the ancient dead, if you like.'

The door opened and Sheridan appeared.

'I know it looks like I'm following you, but I heard you had… oh, wow!' His face lit up as he saw the sarcophagus and he stared at it, trance-like.

'Shed paid for the analysis that's being carried out on Masahanum.'

'Yes, yes, it will be fascinating, I'm sure. It will be like he is speaking to us, there will be so much we can learn. This is the first time he's been removed from his coffin, and we wanted to understand his current condition. He'll have a CT scan and be stabilised for future travel. After that, we'll arrange for him to be returned to a museum in Egypt. He was very forward thinking, you know, Masahanum. He was a philosopher, but died far too young. I've been close to him, and this sarcophagus, many times, but it never stops being thrilling.'

He was beaming, and appeared to be in constant motion. It was actually really lovely to watch.

'I'll be very sad to see him leave, but it's important that he's returned to the country he came from.'

After a little more oohing and aahing from Sheridan, Mark gave me a brief tour of his office, but there was nothing that could compare with Masahanum's sarcophagus.

'Come on, we'll go and get a coffee, I need to see sunlight. I feel like I haven't left here for days. Well, Bill would argue I haven't and I'll need to make it up to him.'

Bill, Mark's husband, had already joked to me that he was enjoying the peace and quiet while Mark was working long hours preparing the exhibition, but I wasn't going to shatter his illusions.

3

The museum café was, strictly speaking, a horsebox with a hole cut in the side, located in a small courtyard next to the street. It couldn't have been more different to the cafés I ran at Charleton House – an architectural display of Baroque opulence and power, and the home of the Fitzwilliam-Scott family for over 500 years.

A sweet old dear behind the counter surprised me by producing a perfect latte, with all the banging, steaming and art of a hipster barista a quarter of her age. A lesson in never judging a book by its cover, or its blue rinse. She had probably also made the carrot cake which I was devouring, Mark watching the process wide-eyed.

'Whoa, Nelly, would you like me to get you a shovel? Make the job easier.'

I wiped a blob of cream cheese frosting from the corner of my mouth. 'I might need to give her a job, this is good.'

'You don't say. I was getting the distinct impression that it was the worst thing you'd ever tasted. Ananya, over here.' Mark waved at an attractive young woman who was making her way towards us, clutching a pile of books. 'Ananya, this is Sophie,

Head of Catering at Charleton House. She runs the cafés, amongst other things, and is currently plotting to steal the staff from here.' He nodded in the direction of the elderly woman, who was now clearing a table and balancing so many dirty plates that it made me nervous. But they all made it back into the horsebox without incident.

'Mimi? She is a bit of a star. Nice to meet you, Sophie, I've heard a lot about you.'

I groaned. 'What's he been saying?'

'No, no, it's all good. He's not so keen on your cat, though.'

I laughed. 'How on earth did you end up talking about Pumpkin?'

'There's a collection of stuffed domestic cats in the museum, a huge array of breeds. Mark commented that he could add to the collection overnight if Lord Eyre ever wished to expand it.'

I gave Mark a vicious glare.

'Join us,' Mark said to Ananya, nodding in the direction of an empty seat.

'I'd love to, but I need to get back to Berwick to deliver a couple of tours. The day job continues apace. I'll be back later, will you still be here?'

'Of course, I've brought a hip flask, a sleeping bag and a photograph of my husband.'

'You'll be sorry when it's all over,' replied Ananya.

'When it's all over, I'm going to sleep solidly for twenty-four hours. Then I'll miss it.'

'Lovely to meet you, Sophie, hope to see you at the opening reception.' I watched Ananya walk away, her shiny black ponytail swinging like a metronome as she moved swiftly between the tables.

'Mark dear, I was just checking, it was 100 cupcakes you wanted for the reception?' The non-hipster barista was resting a hand on Mark's shoulder.

'Yes, perfect. Thanks, Mimi.'

The elderly lady smiled at me. 'I hope you enjoyed the cake, dear.'

'I did, thank you. The coffee was also excellent.'

'Glad to hear it. I've just mastered the heart in the foam, I'm now working on a cat's face.' Her smile widened even further, and then she left us and continued to clear tables. I made the smile I had returned in her direction re-form into a scowl as I turned to Mark, receiving a distinctly nervous expression in return.

'You asked someone else to bake your cakes?'

'Well, I...'

'For the reception, which will be attended by the Duke and Duchess. Our Duke and Duchess. You didn't think to ask me?'

'No, well, Mimi...'

'Mimi is about 100 years old and if whacking the coffee portafilter like that doesn't kill her, baking all those cakes probably will. Apart from the fact that your best friend caters events for the Duke and Duchess on a regular basis and could present you with 100 beautiful cupcakes with a click of her finger...'

'Well, the click of someone else's finger. You don't do all the baking yourself....'

'That's hardly relevant, you know I'd have had them made for you. What are they, sweet little butterfly cakes with vanilla icing? Tasty, but boring to look at?'

'No, actually, they'll all have the head portion of the sarcophagus on them. She made one for me to be sure I approved. It was a work of art.'

I huffed before swigging the remains of my coffee.

'Well, don't come crying to me if the exertion of making 100 gives the poor woman a heart attack and you have to carry the guilt for the rest of your days.'

I formed the best expression of sulk I could muster and wondered how much effort would be required to stuff Mark's body into Masahanum's sarcophagus.

4

'Good morning, sunshine.'

'Sophie, what on earth are you doing here?'

I usually start my day with a view of the sun rising over the magnificent Charleton House, but this morning, I had driven over to the Pilston Museum to surprise Mark.

'Lovely to see you, too.' Mark hadn't tied his bow tie, and although his moustache had a perfect curl on each end, his eyes gave away just how tired he was. 'Bill told me you'd had a late one, so I thought you might need a few things to get you through the day. It's also to show that I've forgiven you for asking Mimi to make the cakes for tonight.'

I followed Mark into the museum, swinging the basket of goodies. 'I've made sure there's enough for Ananya too. You have a flask of coffee, sandwiches for lunch, several home-baked cakes and biscuits, which you'll find are particularly delicious, light, delicate of flavour...' I glanced up at that point.

'I thought you said you'd forgiven me.'

'I have, but if Mimi fails to deliver...'

'You'll what? Dash to M&S because of the short notice?'

'Yeah, probably... some fruit, which I fully expect to still be in there when you return the basket, unless Ananya is healthier than you. Bottles of water and a half bottle of champagne for the two of you to enjoy and have a little private celebration before everyone arrives this evening.'

Mark stopped in front of a solid wooden door and turned to give me a kiss on the cheek. 'You're a star, thank you.' He pushed the door open and flicked on a light, illuminating a gallery with a row of waist-height display cases. They contained a multitude of Egyptian objects from within Masahanum's tomb: small statues, model boats, jewellery, an iron dagger with an ornately decorated sheath, a pair of golden sandals, jars that had contained wine, all of which were meant to assist him in the afterlife. In a corner was a mock-up of a study, which would have looked right at home in Berwick Hall. I knew it had been created using the actual furniture from the study of Lord Decimus Eyre, which had been tucked away under dust sheets for years. I recognised a large photograph of the ninth Duke of Ravensbury, a jovial-looking chap whose waistline gave away just how much he enjoyed parties and dining.

'Last night was hell. A load of plaster fell off the wall, some of the information panels had errors on them and the curtains for the back of that study still hadn't arrived, but Mimi offered to make some overnight…'

'Is there anything she can't do?'

'Well, she wasn't waiting for me in the museum car park with a beautiful basket of goodies, unlike my sweet friend.'

'Give it time, she's probably on her way with a banquet in the back of the car along with the curtains.'

'Now, now. You take a look, I'll just put this in the kitchen and see if Ananya's arrived.'

He disappeared down the corridor and I explored the gallery. It wasn't a large room, but the exhibition was a temporary one that would only be running for six months. The dark wood of the cases sucked out a lot of the sunlight that streamed in through a line of windows close to the ceiling. If anything, the gloom added to the atmosphere – the sense of digging back in time through someone's private collection, which was exactly what this exhibition was.

A number of the glass cases were still open, stands awaiting the precious objects that they would house. Packing boxes were scattered around. The sarcophagus had been moved through, but remained on a wooden pallet, awaiting the delicate handling required to put it on display. The painted eyes of the Egyptian prince stared up at the ceiling, the gold leaf reflecting the light.

The lid of the sarcophagus had been moved, leaving a gap of a couple of inches, making its role as a receptacle of a human body, and not just an attractive object, even clearer. As I stood by its feet, thinking about the young man who had been so carefully placed inside, I heard the door behind me open as Mark returned and examined a glass case next to me.

'Oh good, Ananya got the display of archaeological tools finished. Once Mimi gets here, I can finish the re-creation of Lord Eyre's study, and then when Richard and Suzy arrive, they will put the sarcophagus into position.'

'I see you've changed your mind,' I said.

'About what?' Mark was picking up empty cardboard boxes, breaking them down and making a pile in the corner. 'I knew I'd regret not tidying up last night, but we were just too tired.'

'Putting Masahanum himself on display, his actual body. That must have been an interesting discussion.'

'No, no change. He'll be away for some time.' Mark moved on to stuffing the cardboard into big bags, ready to go out to the skip I'd seen around the corner of the building when I'd arrived.

'But he's still inside.'

Mark gave a low chuckle. 'No, he's not. The lid probably moved as they carried it in here. That, or he found his way back home, hitched a lift.'

'Mark, take a look, I can see the bandages.' I peered into the crack left by the skew-whiff lid. 'See?'

Mark stood next to me, then he bent down and got closer.

'I don't understand. Help me move this.'

'You want me to lift the lid? Don't be ridiculous, I'm not trained. Shouldn't I be wearing gloves or something?'

'Just shift the damn thing, far enough that we can see in properly.'

The instruction was a clear, firm command, not something I heard often from Mark. I did as I was told. We carefully lifted the lid a little, enough to be able to move it, and then turned it, opening the gap. I was terrified of dropping it.

Inside was a mummy, the kind a child might draw. It wasn't exactly wrapped in strips of thin cloth, but a sheet of some kind bound it – a sheet that looked rather new. The head, however, wasn't covered. The sheet had slipped away, revealing not the mummified remains of an Egyptian prince, who would now be well over 3,000 years old, but the grey hair and skin of a person whose most recent birthday had been sometime in the last year. He was familiar looking, but in the shadows of the sarcophagus and with the sheet hiding part of his face, I couldn't place him.

'Was he meant to be a surprise at the reception tonight? You know, like having someone leap out of a birthday cake?' I knew my gallows humour was inappropriate, but was unable to think of anything else to say. Mark's brow creased and he leant closer to the man who was bundled up like a well-swaddled baby.

'No, he was no surprise, everyone knew he was on the guest list. That's Sheridan Tasker.'

5

Mark and I were sitting in my car, takeout cups of coffee getting cold in our hands. We watched as Detective Sergeant Colette Harnby chatted to a couple of the scene of crime officers dressed head to toe in their white space-suits, only their eyes visible above the masks they wore. Drops of rain hit the windscreen of the car, trying desperately to turn into a downpour, but failing and remaining a light shower. Still, it seemed appropriate for the mood of the morning.

'He was such a nice man,' said Mark glumly.

'Why did he like to be called Shed, do you know?'

'Apparently, his older brother called him that when they were children and it stuck. Nothing more than that. Despite the international reputation of his biscuits and all his money, he was very down to earth. He's been supportive and showed a lot of interest in the exhibition from the beginning. Mind you, he's shown a lot of interest in everything to do with the museum, but then there's plenty going on with the plans for the renovation and the building of a new education centre. The museum successfully bid for a substantial amount of money for the project, and Shed sponsored it with a large donation himself. It will have to be closed for around a year when the work is taking place.'

I was about to ask him more questions, but I spotted DS Harnby walking towards the car and wound my window down. She bent down to speak to us.

'Mark, Sophie, how are you doing?'

Mark replied, 'Fine, thank you.' I just nodded; I had a mouthful of coffee.

'Are you feeling up to giving formal statements? I know you've spoken to Joe briefly.' Joe Greene, or rather Detective Constable Greene, was Mark's brother-in-law.

'Yes.' Mark reached for the door handle.

'Hang fire, how about you head down to the station in an hour or so, but give Joe a call first and check there's someone there to see you?'

Mark nodded. Harnby turned her attention solely on me.

'Any questions, Sophie?'

'Me? Why? What?'

'Well, you've probably given the murder some thought and have a number of questions to ask before you reveal who the killer was.' She was trying to fight a smile.

'So, it was murder, then?'

'He hardly rolled himself up in a sheet, then managed to crawl into the coffin like a beige slug...'

'Sarcophagus,' interrupted Mark. Harnby ignored him. I raised my hands in the air in mock surrender, my coffee cup held precariously by a finger and thumb.

'I'm an innocent bystander who simply stumbled across the body while minding her own business. I will, of course, head to the station with Mark later and make a formal statement, and then I will leave the investigation in your very capable hands.'

Harnby gave an almost imperceptible nod, then stood up and turned to leave before coming to an abrupt stop. She looked up at the sky and spoke loudly enough for us to hear.

'What on earth? I can't believe it!'

Mark and I both leaned forward in our seats, looking at the sky through the front windscreen.

'What? I don't see anything,' said Mark as I twisted and turned my head, trying to get a better view.

'Just some flying pigs,' said Harnby before striding off across the tarmac without a backward glance.

'You should have seen your face. Harnby got you.' Mark gave what could only be described as a giggle.

'I hadn't done or said a single thing that was worthy of that comment.' I knew I sounded whiny, but I did feel it was undeserved. Joe looked at me from over his glass of beer.

'You were within yards of a dead body and she has met you before. You do have quite a reputation, and a well-deserved one at that.' Joe had dropped round to Mark and Bill's on his way home. It was late, but he wanted to see if we were okay, and if either of us had remembered anything else since we'd given our statements at the station. I decided not to argue. He was right on both counts.

'Tell me more about Shed Tasker, Mark. You met him a few times?'

Mark nodded. 'As soon as we got to the installation stage, I saw quite a lot of him. The museum is receiving funding to go ahead with a major overhaul, so it will be closed for at least a year, probably more like eighteen months, and Shed was at the forefront of the campaign. They got a lot of money from the Arts Council England, the National Lottery Heritage Fund, and a number of private donations, of which Shed's own donation was the largest. He and Elliot Knight made quite a team – Shed the go-getting entrepreneur who could talk numbers, Elliot the slightly bumbling old-school museum director, an act, I'm sure of it – with vast amounts of passion and knowledge about the place. The money came pouring in.'

'So they got on?' Joe asked.

'Yes, very well. I imagine Elliot is rather upset.'

'He is, and bumbling is the right word. He could hardly speak when I saw him. He kept cleaning his glasses with a handkerchief and repeating *I don't understand, I don't understand.* Well, if there's nothing else you can tell me, I should get going. Harnby wants us all in the office for a 7am briefing.'

Bill showed his brother out while Mark and I remained slumped on the sofa.

'Tell me more about Shed.'

'Can't resist, can you? Harnby was spot on. Okay, Sheridan Tasker. Mid-sixties, married, a couple of children. I gave Shed and his wife a tour a few weeks ago, she's as nice as he is. Made his fortune with a biscuit company, which he then sold for some eye-watering sum of money. Always been passionate about the local community and has made donations to all sorts of organisations over the years, everything from the scout group to providing university scholarships for school-leavers. It's his name emblazoned across the front of the local football team's strip.'

I knew I'd seen the name recently, beyond a packet of biscuits, and that must have been it. The local paper pictured the team on the front page after they'd won a regional amateur championship, the words *Tasker Foundation* written large across the players' chests.

'So not someone you'd expect to get murdered?'

'I wouldn't go that far. He'd made millions, he must have hacked off a few people to get where he did. Maybe someone wanted money for something and he refused to give it. Perhaps he'd bad-mouthed someone while enjoying a particularly expensive bottle of malt whisky.'

'So, he was a drinker?'

'No – I don't know – it was just an example. Could he have angered someone enough to make them want to kill him? Very possibly. None of us are perfect. I'm sure a few people have got a voodoo doll that looks like me tucked away. Actually, that might explain my bad back.' He leant forward and rubbed his lower back as if to emphasise his point.

'Well, you can't blame me, I've been sticking the pins into your legs.' I grinned, but Mark shook his head.

'It's probably Joyce, I imagine she has a collection of them, each riddled with pins.'

I laughed. 'And each with a perfect little bow tie and a tiny waxed moustache.'

Joyce Brocklehurst ran all the gift shops at Charleton House, and she and Mark had a famously volatile friendship, but there was affection at the heart of it. At least, there could be, but it might require a team of archaeologists to be certain. Joyce was currently on holiday in Scotland with a friend and it had been extremely quiet at work – make that peaceful – without the two of them bickering all day long.

'So long as she's had the little outfits tailor-made, I don't mind.'

We sat in silence for a while, each of us deep in our own thoughts. Eventually, I stood up.

'I should go, it's gone eleven. Pumpkin will be wondering where I am and she hasn't had her dinner.'

'Then I should take personal protection, or you'll be the next dead body that Joe has to investigate. Not that she couldn't do with skipping a meal or two – I swear she's bigger every time I see her.'

'I'll leave you to tell her she needs to go on a diet.'

Mark shook his head. 'Not a chance, I don't have a death wish.'

6

Mark held his audience in speechless rapture as he told and retold the story of finding Shed Tasker's body in the museum. The interest in him was less surprising now that he was a celebrity of sorts, his own weekly history slot on the local TV news having been extended indefinitely. In his telling of the previous day's events, you'd think that I hadn't been there, but I didn't mind. My ability to trip over dead bodies was hardly something I wanted to list on my CV.

If it hadn't been for Mark and his groupies, made up from other Charleton House staff, the Library Café would have been deserted. Or rather, our customers would have been scattered around the room instead of moving a lot of the chairs to surround him as if he were a moustachioed deity. It was so early in the day, paying visitors hadn't made it far enough into the house to reach this café, with its book-lined walls, armchairs you could sink into in front of a large ornate fireplace, and wooden tables and chairs. It had been furnished to look a little like the Duke's luxurious library, and indeed, he had been involved in the design. The naturally dark space was cosy rather than gloomy, and it was my favourite of the three cafés I had responsibility for.

The museum and Shed's body seemed a million miles away, and this morning, I rather liked that.

'So, you found another corpse. What is it with you and the dearly departed?' It seemed my moment of escaping reality was over almost as quickly as it had begun.

'Morning, Tina. So you've heard?'

'Of course I've heard. The team could gossip for England, despite me advising them against it.' Tina, who worked as the supervisor of the Library Café, was smiling broadly. I might be her boss, but I could hardly penalise her for telling the truth about my habit of stumbling across the dead.

'I don't know what all the fuss is about. I mean, it's a shame someone died, but that place is a nightmare to work at.'

I looked up at the speaker and groaned inwardly. A notoriously awkward individual who worked in the ticket office, Sharon Porter was forever having run-ins with the HR department. She'd had more time off sick in recent months than I'd had in my career to date, with questionable explanations, and she disagreed with everything management said or did. I'd turned her down for supervisor roles twice; I was surprised she was still talking to me.

'What do you mean, a nightmare? I've only ever heard good things about it,' I replied. Sharon huffed. With that one exhalation of air, she managed to make it sound like I was as stupid as everyone else she'd been unfortunate enough to encounter today.

'Well, you would think that. You don't know anyone who works there.'

'Mark was working there.'

'That's different, he was temporary. He wasn't embedded in the day-to-day.'

'And you *do* know someone, I take it.'

'My brother Kit. I know all about working there.'

I tried not to laugh. If Kit was anything like his sister, it was probably he who was the nightmare, not the museum.

'So, why doesn't he leave?' It was a question I'd always wanted to ask Sharon too, but never had the nerve to.

'Dedication, plain and simple. They don't appreciate everything he brings to the role, and they'd do well to listen to him. He's worked there most of his life and if anyone knows what's good for the organisation, it's him. Besides which, we Porters don't give up, it's not in our nature. If something is worth fighting for, then that's exactly what we'll do. Now, if you wouldn't mind hurrying up with my coffee, I have a meeting with HR in five minutes and I don't want to be late.'

Poor HR, I thought, making a mental note to send them a tray of chocolate brownies in a couple of hours. They'd need all the sustenance, sympathy and support available after that meeting.

7

'Sophie, good morning. I was wondering if you had a moment?' Alexander Fitzwilliam-Scott, the twelfth Duke of Ravensbury, had walked into the café.

'Can I get you a coffee?'

'No, no, thank you, Sophie. I just wanted a quick word.' He folded himself into a chair and crossed his legs, revealing a pair of lemon yellow socks under his navy blue suit trousers. His pale blue shirt was open at the neck and he wasn't wearing a tie. He was the perfect vision of off-duty aristocracy, but despite his laid-back position, he didn't look entirely relaxed.

'I feel a little awkward asking you about this as it's the sort of thing I've advised you against getting involved with. Only, I've been made aware that you were at the Pilston Museum yesterday.'

He paused, waiting for an answer.

'I was, yes.'

'Right, well, I've also been told that you and Mark found Sheridan Tasker. His body, I mean.'

I looked across at Mark and he caught my eye. The group that had gathered about him was thinning out and he was collecting up his things. He gave me a look that I translated as *should I join you?* I returned what I hoped was a subtle shake of the head. I'd got the impression the Duke wanted our conversation to be as discreet as possible. Joining me in the café made it look like a casual chat; coming to my office or calling me to meet him elsewhere would have brought attention to it.

'Yes, that's correct. Did you know him?'

'I did, yes. The Duchess and I have known the couple for years. His wife, Harriet, went to school with my sister and I met Sheridan at a fundraising event for a conservation charity. They're extremely good company – in fact, we were going to suggest they join us at the house in London for a weekend…'

He disappeared into his thoughts for a moment before seeming to remember that I was there.

'Look, Sophie, I know I've made it clear that I think it unwise for you to take an interest in a police investigation…'

Especially when the end result is that your son is handed a prison sentence, I thought.

'…but did you get the impression that it was something they might be able to resolve quickly? Were there a lot of clues around? It's just that our mothers were friends. Barbara Tasker is still alive. She's in her nineties, rather frail, and when I visit her this afternoon, I'd like to be able to tell her something that might make this awful tragedy a little easier to bear, such as he didn't suffer, or the police are soon likely to apprehend the killer.'

I wondered why he was asking me and not Detective Inspector Flynn, Harnby's boss, but I remembered that the Duke never liked to be seen to pull in favours.

'I'm afraid I can't answer either of those questions. He was largely hidden by the sheet that had been wrapped around him, so I don't even know how he died, and as for the crime scene, it was a bit of a mess anyway. Mark and Ananya, along with a couple of museum staff, were still setting up the exhibition and it was very much a work in progress.'

'Right, I see.'

He vanished into his thoughts again and we sat there in a silence that became more and more uncomfortable.

'Well, thank you, Sophie.' The Duke stood. 'I appreciate your time. I'll be off, then.'

He was a man that currently embodied the word *discombobulated*. I put it down to the shock, or the thought of going to see Shed's mother. I decided to expel it from my mind and concentrate on the business of running three cafés and catering for a number of upcoming events. That was enough to be getting on with.

8

'I wondered how long it would take for you to turn up.' I grinned at Detective Constable Joe Greene. 'Coffee, detective?'

'And a cake, and five minutes of your time, please.'

'I am popular today, I've got men queuing up to spend time with me.'

Joe looked a little confused, then it quickly got uncomfortable. There had been a time when it looked like we would end up dating, but it wasn't to be and we had never really spoken about it. Still, I had strayed onto that subject with my attempt at humour.

'Grab a seat and I'll join you,' I said, hastily changing the subject and turning to prepare drinks for us both.

'You're keeping us busy,' Joe said a few minutes later, peering over his mug at me as I set a plate with a hearty slice of gingerbread cake on it and my own coffee on the table, and then sat down opposite him.

'I didn't kill him.'

'Are you sure? You're always to be found at the location of a murder victim.'

'After the actual event, yes, I will concede that. But not until they have long since died.'

'Hmm, well, I know where to find you should the pattern become more concerning.' I knew he was joking, but I did sometimes wonder if I was going to find myself the number-one suspect in a case.

'So, how can I help? I'm not going to confess, so we might as well skip that part.'

Joe laughed. 'Well, first of all, I needed a caffeine hit, and one that didn't come from the vending machine at the station and taste like dirty dishwater. Secondly, just a routine visit to ask if you've thought of anything else since you gave us your statement.' He took a large bite out of the thick wedge of gingerbread cake I had cut for him, and watched me as I mulled over the question. Nothing had sprung to mind overnight, and I hadn't thought of anything else as I'd tried to get to sleep.

'I've replayed everything from our arrival through to me spotting the body in the sarcophagus. There was nothing strange outside the museum, and I didn't see anything or anyone that I would have considered unusual inside. But having said that, I don't know the place well. I wouldn't know if someone was the plumber or a suspicious character who shouldn't be in there. I know that some staff had already arrived and were working, and the door I went through to the gallery wasn't locked. I'm guessing that every member of staff has reason to visit the gallery, so fingerprints aren't much use?'

Joe shook his head. 'The gallery has been closed as they set up the new exhibition, but it's usually open to the public, so no, fingerprints aren't much use to us. Anyone who's handled the sarcophagus has been using gloves – apart from you and Mark, of course.' He gave me a pointed look.

'There was a body in there and Mark told me to help lift the lid. I was hardly going to run around looking for a pair of Marigolds, now, was I?'

'Fair point.'

'What about CCTV?'

'The camera was pointing the wrong way. It had been moved, and whoever had done it knew which angle to come from to make sure they weren't seen. Not that the security team would have seen much at the time anyway. They'd put a football match up on one of the monitors and I get the impression they weren't paying much attention to anything else that evening. Someone could have wandered around dressed as a chicken and they wouldn't have noticed.'

'I hope their team won.'

'They didn't. It was a double blow for the hapless lot.'

'I'm sorry I can't be of more help. Do you have anything at all to go on?'

'Not yet. Sheridan was a man of good standing, generous, well respected, but as soon as we start digging beneath the surface, something will come up, and then we'll just follow that trail. One thing you can be sure of, though…'

'What's that?'

'When we do find something below the surface, I won't be telling you about it.'

'Not even for another slice of gingerbread cake?'

'Not even.' He took another bite. 'It is good, though.'

'I'll bake another, I'll be able to break you.'

Joe laughed and crumbs fell out of his mouth.

'There is one thing, though, but I doubt it's anything because the source isn't very reliable.'

'Go on,' Joe said after swallowing.

'One of the ticketing staff here has a brother who works at the museum. She was saying that it's not a great place to work and there are lots of issues. Now, this woman makes a complaint if the wind blows in the wrong direction, and HR staff have been known to hide under their desks when they see her coming, but perhaps there *are* a lot of problems at the museum and her brother is right. If so, then there could be all sorts of issues and seething resentments rumbling around. I don't know what the day-to-day running of things would have to do with the chair of the trustees, but still, there might be a link.'

Joe looked thoughtful. 'Anything else going to miraculously spring to mind before I go?'

'No, that's it. Do you want another slice of cake to take with you?'

'Yes, thank you, and no, I don't owe you.' He gave me the smile of a naughty schoolboy who'd just got one over on his parents.

'We'll see.'

This could go on all day, but I had customers to serve, and a murder to mull over.

9

'I don't know why you wanted to come with me, there won't be anything to see. The gallery is still closed off as a crime scene.' Mark looked across at me as I pulled into the museum car park. 'I take that back, I know exactly why you're here, but I can't imagine that we'll find anything connected with the murder.'

'I agree, but it might be useful to be around the staff, listening to what they have to say.'

Mark smiled. 'That won't be a problem, I doubt anyone is talking about anything else.' I was about to say something complimentary – and sarcastic – about his assessment of human nature when we were interrupted steps away from the museum door.

'Mark Boxer, do you have a moment? Gary Endersley, I'm with the *High Peak Gazette*. Is it right that you found the body of Sheridan Tasker?' The man held his phone out, ready to use it to record anything Mark had to say. He wore a bright blue waterproof hiking jacket and black trousers, his hair fell into his eyes and he didn't look much older than twenty-one.

Mark paused, taken by surprise.

'I'm sure your Friday evening viewers would love to hear more about your experience, and how you're doing,' the journalist continued.

Mark, as though suddenly waking up, said very clearly, 'No comment,' and walked into the museum.

'And how about you? Are you a friend of Mr Boxer's? Has the discovery of a dead body given him a dreadful shock?'

'No comment,' I replied and dashed through the doors to catch up with Mark.

'I have to admit, I didn't expect my first paparazzi experience to be about a murder.' Mark had come to a stop when he was safely into the building. 'I was hoping it would be after getting a BAFTA for best factual series, or because I'd been invited to the next royal wedding.'

I glanced back towards the doors. 'You don't think he's going to follow us in?'

'You won't let him in, will you, Graham?' Mark looked at a tall man in a security guard's uniform who was standing just inside the doors. In my rush to catch up, I hadn't seen him.

'Of course not, Mr Boxer, no one's coming through that door who shouldn't until we open back up to the public.'

'Any idea when that will be?' I asked. Graham shook his head.

'Sorry, Miss, no. I did hear word that the police will probably be out of here in a couple of days. I know that Mr Knight is keen to get back to normal.'

'This must have come as a heck of a shock,' I said to Graham. 'Somewhere like this, a nice little local museum with plenty of security devices.'

'Oh, I wouldn't go that far, Miss. The place is quite old, and so is the security. At night, it's typically just a couple of our chaps and a few cameras, but they're often playing up. I've always worried that something major would happen, but I thought it would be theft, not murder.'

'It does seem difficult to imagine murder here at the museum.

It's such a nice, harmless old place. You must have been giving it a lot of thought.'

I could see Mark giving me a wry smile out of the corner of my eye. He was patiently waiting for me.

'Thought about nothing else. Trying to think who might have wanted Mr Tasker dead. I always liked him, even though he was rather exhausting. Very energetic man. And I know not everyone was happy with the changes that were to take place, but we all knew he had good intentions.'

Graham had raised a valid point – Shed's good intentions were obvious – but it hadn't stopped me from missing the subtext entirely.

'So, there were people who weren't keen on the renovations?'

'Oh, of course, not everyone likes change, and it is a historic place. The new design is rather... well, new.'

'Was there anyone in particular who was against it?' I really hoped that Graham didn't wonder why I might be asking. He appeared to be considering my question quite intently.

'You should have a word with Kit Porter. He started a petition against it. It didn't get anywhere, though, as not many people wanted to sign it, and eventually the building project was signed and sealed and the design appeared in the papers.'

'Thanks, Graham, I will.'

Already, I had a name that had cropped up a couple of times. I wasn't exactly looking forward to talking to Kit, he didn't sound like fun company, but it seemed like a good place to start.

10

The office that Mark shared with Ananya was a windowless box in the basement. Three desks had been pushed together to form one central desk, with two computers and piles of books and papers making it look like the workspace of very active minds, which it was. Mark had been allowed to take a period of leave from his role at Charleton House while he and Ananya put the exhibition together. He'd already dropped down to four days a week so he could fit in the filming for his weekly TV slot, and I was starting to get worried that he wouldn't come back to work, or that he'd return, but other opportunities would come his way and he'd be gone in a year or two. I couldn't imagine working there without him. Apart from anything, I doubted that I could cope with Joyce on my own, and she'd never admit it, but she'd miss him too. Either way, Charleton House just wouldn't be the same without Mark Boxer.

He hasn't left yet, I had to remind myself, *and he may never leave*, I added optimistically, crossing my fingers for added security.

'No Ananya today?'

'No. She didn't get quite so much time off the day job as me, so she'll be back up at Berwick Hall. There's no point her coming in until we get access to the gallery again and can finish everything off.'

Sitting in an old swivel office chair, I aimlessly spun myself to and fro while Mark logged on to a computer. I came to an abrupt stop as the door opened and a man in a tweed jacket and round black-rimmed spectacles stepped into the room.

'Mark, ah, glad you're here, I was hoping you would be.'

Based on the man's appearance alone, I would have said he was some kind of professor, but I happened to recognise him from photographs, so I knew it was Elliot Knight, the museum director. He didn't step all the way into the room and gave the impression of needing to be somewhere else.

'I wanted to see how you were. I believe you had the dreadful experience of discovering poor Sheridan. If there is anything you need?' Elliot appeared uncomfortable, clearly not a man used to expressing his emotions.

'Actually, it was Sophie who found him.' Mark looked over at me and Elliot followed suit. He looked surprised to discover that there was someone else in the room.

'Oh, right, I'm sorry. Hello, you are?'

'Sophie Lockwood, I work with Mark at Charleton House.'

'Oh, you do? Well, it's a dreadful business, just dreadful.' He appeared to have run out of platitudes, but was saved by the appearance of a blonde-haired woman behind him.

'Elliot, do you have a minute?' She looked concerned – nervous, perhaps – and I knew instinctively that she was about to break some bad news to the museum director. He turned to face her, his foot holding the door open, and she spoke directly into his ear. I couldn't catch what she said.

Elliot pulled his head back and stared at her. 'Are you sure?'

'Very. Nimrod Dix came to find you, he's waiting in your office.'

Elliot gave out a groan that sounded as if he'd been punched in the stomach.

'This cannot be happening. He must be mistaken. He has to be.' Elliot walked quickly down the corridor, muttering what sounded like an array of expletives. The woman put her hand out to stop the door slamming and watched him disappear round a corner.

'Nimrod Dix is?' I asked Mark.

'Keeper of the Vogelbach Coin Room. Ashley, what's happened?'

'They're missing,' said the woman, sounding unsure of the words as she spoke them. 'Nimrod says the Lymehill coins are gone, stolen. I should go.'

She followed Elliot's path, the door slamming closed behind her. Mark looked concerned.

'The Lymehill coins are?'

'Incredibly important,' he answered. 'It's a hoard of gold coins found in a field just outside the village of Lymehill in 2002. Fifty of them, late Iron Age and Roman. It was an incredible find by a local man who'd been given a metal detector as a birthday present. It had been intended as a joke. He was always losing tools outside, so it was meant to help him find a hammer that had been in the family for years. He did find it, but not before locating the coins, which he donated to the museum.'

'If they went missing the night of the murder,' I said, 'then you have your motive. The thief must have been disturbed.'

'But why go to the bother of wrapping Shed up and putting him in a sarcophagus? Surely you'd bang him on the back of the head, and then make a run for it. You wouldn't hang around making him look like a Halloween display.'

'The killer made a real effort to ensure Shed was never found, or at least not quickly? He had a very sick and twisted sense of humour?'

Mark had sat in a chair opposite me, his forehead creased in thought.

'There's something entirely logical about it. An extremely

valuable collection is stolen, someone who could have stumbled across the thief at work is found dead in a gallery. But equally, it just doesn't seem like a smash and grab. Too much care was taken to conceal Shed's body, in a sarcophagus that he had always found fascinating. It's as though the killer knew Shed well enough to know what interested him. It feels personal, it doesn't feel like a common or garden robbery.'

I had to agree. 'First of all, we're assuming the coins were stolen on the night of the murder. Second of all, are the coins actually worth stealing? Presumably if the thief tries to sell them, they'll be immediately identifiable and no one will want to touch them.'

'I suggest,' said Mark, 'that we give it about an hour, then we go and talk to Nimrod. See if he's alright, one shocked person to another, and give him some much-needed support.'

11

Nimrod Dix had an office off a corridor of offices, each one behind an unassuming grey plywood door, all needing a lick of paint.

'Let's hope Doctor Dix is decent,' said Mark with a raise of an eyebrow. I looked skywards; I should have guessed a surname like that would have Mark auditioning for a *Carry On* film.

He knocked on the door.

'Come in.'

'Nimrod, hello there.'

'Mark,' Nimrod sighed. 'How can I help? I'm a bit tied up at the moment.' Nimrod was thinning on top – make that almost entirely bald – but big, loose curls circled his head. If it wasn't biologically impossible, I'd have assumed that he'd lost his hair since finding out that the Lymehill coins had disappeared.

'That's why we've come. We wanted to see how you are, if there's anything we can do to help?'

Nimrod didn't even look at me. I seemed to have become invisible since entering the museum. What was it with all these distracted academic types?

'I don't see what you could do, but thank you anyway. I'm

currently phoning everyone I know, asking them to keep an eye out for the coins in case the thief tries to sell them. They'd have to be stupid to try, but then you'd have to be pretty stupid to steal them in the first place. It's pointless.'

'Do you know for sure if they were taken the same night as Shed was killed?'

Nimrod nodded. 'I'd removed a couple for some students to look at and returned them before going home on the day prior to the reception.'

'I take it they're financially valuable? That if they could find a buyer, the thief could get a lot of money for them?'

Nimrod turned to look at me.

'Sorry, this is Sophie, a friend of mine,' explained Mark. Nimrod stared at me, initially looking as though he was confused about my presence in his office, but then his features softened.

'Hello, Sophie, apologies, we meet at a rather stressful time. They're worth around a million pounds, but you'd never be able to find a buyer.'

'What about a private collector who doesn't intend to tell anyone they have them, they just want to possess them?'

'Then you could almost name your price. Collectors like that, who want to own something for the sake of owning it, who are concerned with how powerful and special it makes them feel, usually have vast amounts of money and will pay almost anything to get what they want. But the Lymehill Hoard isn't really in that league.'

'Was there anything contentious about the museum having it?'

'In what way?'

'I don't know – was the family who found the coins reluctant to part with them? Did another museum want them? Was there some doubt over their provenance?'

Nimrod shook his head. 'Not that I'm aware of, and I was here at the time, although I wasn't keeper. As far as I recall, it was all very simple. As soon as the landowner found them, he called the museum hoping we could identify them for him.'

'And he didn't want any money?' That surprised me. Even if it was a couple of thousand rather than the million they were worth, most people would have wanted something.

'No. He was a local man who said they were the property of the community.' Nimrod pressed his fingers against his temples and sighed. 'At least there are *some* good people in the world.'

It all sounded simple enough. Landowner found coins, landowner donated coins to museum. Someone liked sparkly gold things and decided to steal coins.

'What was his name, the landowner?' I was following Mark back down to the basement.

'Can't remember, but it will be easy enough to check.' He stopped. 'I have an idea.'

'Do you need a lie down?'

'To think I was about to suggest we go and have coffee. But we don't have to, it's fine. I have work to do and you can go back to Charleton House and sell chocolate brownies to screaming toddlers and exhausted mothers.'

He started walking again, but I remained where I was. He eventually realised I wasn't following and turned around.

'I'll see you up there, and be nice to Mimi if you see her.'

Mimi had her hands full. Not everyone watched the news every day and there were quite a few people arriving at the museum unaware that it would be closed due to my gruesome discovery. In most cases, they chose to have a drink while deciding what to do next. There were already a number of cake stands which contained nothing more than a handful of crumbs, but Mimi kept up her friendly banter with a smile on her face and no sign that she was flagging. I was beginning to wonder if she was some kind of robot – that and if it really might be possible to poach her and give her a job at Charleton House.

I took a picnic table that was tucked away in a far corner of the area, mindful of the journalist who had put in an appearance this morning. Chances were he wouldn't be the last. This time, however, the worst that happened was a few people watching Mark walk towards me, then turning to their friends to discuss whether or not that was really 'him'.

'Did you get the name of the landowner who found the Lymehill Hoard? I think we should pay him a visit, find out a bit more. It could be that someone has contacted him, wondering if he kept any back.'

'I did, Ralph Jones. He's about thirty minutes' drive from here. I had a quick look online and in all the interviews he did, he came across as very friendly, so I don't think we'll have any difficulty getting him to talk to us. I'm assuming the police or the museum have told him about the theft, or we might need to be prepared to be the bearers of bad news.'

'Unless he decided to take them back,' I suggested.

'Do you really think he would do that?'

'Maybe he had a change of heart, wanted to keep them in the family. He could need the money, and so stole them in order to sell them. He must have had people contact him in the early days and offer to buy them off him for cash instead of him donating them.'

'He's not allowed to sell them, not legally. You're meant to report the find to the coroner and then there's all sorts of legalities involving them being retained by the Crown. He could get an unlimited fine or even a stint in prison if he hadn't reported them, and once they were mentioned in the press there was no way he could try and sell them.'

'That doesn't stop people asking, and if he stole them and got away with it then he could sell them to a private collector who would also keep quiet about it.'

Mark nodded. 'But would he really go to such elaborate lengths to hide the body of someone who disturbed him? That still doesn't sit right with me.'

We sat in silence, each of us deep in thought. After a while, I spoke.

'Why are we doing this? Digging into another murder. I have a job to do, so do you.'

Mark raised his eyebrows at my question. 'Not so much, not until the police let us back into the gallery and we can finish setting up.'

'Yes, but that's only going to be a couple of days. After that, you're going to be full steam ahead with the opening and all the press interviews, plus you've still got filming scheduled.'

'If you want something doing, ask a busy person.'

'True, but the police are busy people, so I reckon they can solve it.'

Mark grinned at me. 'Yeah, but isn't it fun when we solve it first?'

'It's not a competition, and anyway, I like to think of it as assisting the police with their investigations.'

'Whatever it is…' said Mark as he watched a young woman make a beeline for us, and then pulled out his pocket watch '…it'll have to wait. That's the museum's press officer and I've just remembered I'm meant to be doing a phone interview about the exhibition right this minute.'

He grimaced at me, mouthed *sorry* at the woman and unwound his long legs from under the picnic table.

'I won't be long, then we can continue to *not* compete with the police.'

12

Ralph Jones lived on a small farm. The main house and the cottage next to it were immaculately kept. A beautiful cottage garden surrounded both buildings, a theme of pinks and purples clearly intentionally sown into the display, and the delicate flowers bobbed and waved in the breeze. Small, worn stone statues were scattered about, drawing the eye to examine the area more closely. The figures were in various states of disrepair, and looked like they had been cleaned and given a home having been found elsewhere. The two farm buildings further up looked well used. There was plenty of mud at that end of the driveway, but they were well maintained nonetheless.

Mark and I had waited at a gate to be buzzed in, although that made it sound grander than it was. As I parked, an older man with a salt-and-pepper beard walked out to meet us. He was good looking in a weather-beaten way, his clothes well worn.

'Sorry about this,' he said as he glanced down at his clothing. 'I've just been working on one of the tractors. Come on in.'

We followed him into a modern kitchen, all white with a slate floor. It didn't look quite finished. The furniture was all in place, but it needed a bit more work to make it feel homely, like a kitchen should. He put the kettle on as he told us about the farm. His parents lived in the small cottage while he and his wife lived here in the main building, a barn that had only recently been converted, with their two sons.

'It was a long-running joke that I was forever losing my tools and they could end up anywhere. As soon as I bought a replacement, the old one would turn up, so the family all chipped in and got me a metal detector. It was an expensive joke, but I ended up quite liking it. Didn't expect to find buried treasure, though.' He laughed and his entire face crinkled. 'Quite a shock, it was.'

'It was very kind of you to give it to the museum,' I said. 'Were you not tempted to keep it?'

Ralph poured boiling water into three mugs without asking what we wanted to drink. Tea it would have to be, then. I could always try to find a houseplant to water with it when his back was turned.

'It was the property of those who had come before, and they weren't alive to ask. The coins weren't mine to sell. I figure they're doing more good in the museum where kids can learn from them. Or at least, they could. If I get my hands on whoever took them...' His words trailed off and he buried his face in his mug of tea.

'Did you have anyone offer to buy them off you, privately, once word got out?' Mark asked.

'Oh aye, a couple of phone calls. But by the time the press knew about the discovery, I'd already agreed to donate them to the museum, and it's not allowed anyway.'

'Do you remember who those people were? Did you take any details?'

'The police asked me the same question,' he said, looking intently at Mark. 'Do you think one of them decided to get their hands on the coins another way?'

'I really don't know, but it's a possibility.'

'Aye, it stands to reason if someone's desperate to get them, but no. I don't remember anything 'bout the people that phoned. I couldn't even tell you if they were men or women, but I'm pretty sure they were all men. I think having a woman call would have stood out.'

'Why's that?' I asked, out of genuine curiosity.

'Oh, I don't know, I suppose it's harder to imagine a woman being interested in old coins. More of a bloke's hobby.'

I had no idea if that was true, but I would have made the same assumption.

'Did anyone local show an unusual amount of interest? Was there anyone who didn't want you to donate them?' The thief could have come from anywhere, but it would be handy if they were from around here. I also wanted to enquire whether any of his family members were against the idea of giving the coins away, but I instinctively liked Ralph and didn't want to say anything that could be tantamount to asking if one of his loved ones had stolen them. I clearly would never have made a good police officer.

Ralph shook his head again. 'People were interested. I had a lot of them asking if they could borrow the metal detector, all hoping to find treasure in the bottom of their garden, but they didn't want to buy the coins. They just wanted the same luck as me.'

It had been foolish to hope that we would walk away from Ralph's with a name that would lead us straight to the killer, but it was worth a try. Not having the name of someone who had been desperate to get their hands on the coins when they had been discovered, left anyone who had ever heard of the hoard and liked the idea of owning it as a potential suspect, which probably brought the list to a number somewhere in the thousands, if not millions. And they could live anywhere in the world.

This was an avenue that I was happy to leave to the police to explore.

'Do you believe him?' Mark asked as we got back in my car.

'I do. I like him, he seems a genuinely nice bloke.' I turned the key in the ignition and looked over at the door to the smaller of the barns. I was sure I had seen someone duck inside to avoid my stare, and I was sure they had been there when we arrived too. I believed Ralph, but I didn't know anything about the rest of his family.

13

'The egg order is going to be late; the van broke, but none of the eggs did. The light in the sandwich fridge is on the blink again, literally. Mark has been in here asking after you, twice – I think he's bored – and Ryan called to say did you get the message he left on your mobile phone yesterday?'

Tina finished reeling off the list of issues I was faced with, having just got back from a meeting with the marketing department about Christmas. All I could think about was coffee. The energy burst provided by my one and only coffee of the day so far was coming to the end of its efficacy.

'And Chelsea is making you a coffee, which will be here right about… now.'

Chelsea handed me a latte. I'd have kissed her if I had the energy, and wasn't afraid of a harassment complaint being brought against me. I didn't reply. I knew that Tina hadn't finished.

'I had Craig head out and get some eggs to tide us over, maintenance say they'll have the lightbulb fixed by the end of the day, and I've plugged in your mobile phone, which you left in the office last night, so you should have enough charge to pick up your messages by now.'

I thought for a moment, then stopped thinking. Too much effort.

'I'm not sure what to say to all of that. There's *thank you* obviously, but it needs more. It's impressive, and yet oddly obsessive. I also wonder if you're after my job, which quite frankly, you could do in your sleep and without a gallon of coffee, so I'm a little afraid. Afraid that I'll be unemployed and won't be able to feed Pumpkin. Once the starvation starts to kick in, which for her will take about two hours, she'll look at me hungrily, and before I know it, I'll meet an untimely demise being consumed by my fat tabby cat, and all because you're so bloody efficient. Which makes you a killer, Tina Stott. A cold-blooded killer.'

Even I knew I'd gone a bit far. Tina gave me a look which indicated she was worried for my sanity and walked away. Chelsea stared at me, but remained where she was.

'Do you want me to get you a decaf?'

I pretended to spit on the floor. 'Don't use such foul language in my presence.'

She smirked and walked off.

Ryan, I thought as I walked into my office. I hadn't spoken to Ryan since before I'd found Sheridan Tasker's body. If he had read about the incident and seen Mark's name in the article, he would have known that his female colleague – as I hoped I had been described, if I got a mention at all – was me. He was probably worried.

Ryan was a historian-cum-TV-presenter-cum-author who I had started dating sporadically a few months ago. I'd already met his mother, but that was before he'd asked me out, so it didn't count on the relationship-progression charts. We'd been out for dinner twice; both occasions had been very nice, but that was it.

Right now, he was on a book tour around the country and was due to fly to America in a few weeks to do book signings over there. He basically had the career that Mark wanted, only without the ornate moustache or love for pocket watches. But, he was incredibly cute and he seemed to enjoy my company. I wasn't entirely sure where I wanted our relationship to go, but I did know that the first call I was going to make was to him.

Bother! It went to his voicemail, and annoyingly, he hadn't recorded a personalised message so I didn't even get to hear his voice. I left Ryan a message telling him that I'd been reunited with my mobile phone and to call me.

'Is it safe to come in?' There was another cute male voice, only this was one that belonged to Joe Greene.

'I honestly can't answer that,' I said, 'but I am afraid of Tina, so I reckon it's safer in here than out there.'

Joe looked at me with a very quizzical expression. 'Do you want to drink a bit more of that,' he nodded at my latte, 'and then we can have a proper conversation?'

I took a large gulp, burning my mouth in the process. 'Done. What is it?'

'Message from Harnby. Stay away from anyone who has a link to dead bodies or ancient coins.'

'That's going to be very difficult. We all have a link to someone who has died within living memory, unless we're about two years old, and even then it's a distinct possibility, plus my cousin used to work at a funeral home, so am I not allowed to see him ever again? Also, how ancient is ancient? I believe the Duke inherited a coin collection, but it's not worth much. Old, yes, ancient, not sure, and I have a meeting with him tomorrow. Should I cancel it?'

'Have you finished?'

I made a mental note to get more sleep, but didn't answer his question. I drank more coffee instead.

'You were spotted driving away from Ralph Jones's farm and

I'm guessing you weren't there to go gambolling with the goats. Harnby is annoyed.'

'More annoyed than usual?'

'Does it matter?'

'It might determine how much attention I pay to her demands.'

'Very annoyed. She's particularly stressed and I don't know why. There's something weird going on and I'm starting to wonder if she's applied for a job somewhere else.' Joe perched on the edge of my desk. There wasn't room for a second chair in my office – there was barely room for the one I was sitting on. He looked downbeat.

'Would that be a problem?'

'I guess not, in the grand scheme of things. We all have careers, people come and go. I'll work with lots of sergeants over the course of my career.'

'And you'll be one soon enough. Now you've passed your exam, you just need to find a vacancy and apply for it.'

'True, but I like working with her. She's good at her job and I know where I am with her. She's straight talking. Bit of a stickler for the rules, but there's nothing wrong with that.'

I looked at the coffee cup he was holding. 'She'd make you pay for that for a start,' I said with a smile.

'She would.'

'On the upside, if Harnby goes, that leaves her job vacant and you'd be a shoo-in, I'm sure of it. You could be a sergeant and remain here.'

'I did think of that,' he replied with a lopsided grin. 'Silver linings and all that. Anyway, that's not why I dropped round. It was to deliver the message to mind your own business, which I have now delivered and which I'm sure you'll ignore, but Harnby can't say I didn't try.'

'Good man. Your powers of deduction and observation are a perfect illustration of why you'll make an excellent sergeant.'

He started to leave.

'Gambolling.' That stopped him in his tracks.

'What?'

'Gambolling. Good word that, gambolling.' I said it slowly, enjoying the shape of the word in my mouth. 'Gambolling.'

'You really need to cut down on the caffeine.' And with that, he left.

14

After Joe had left, I spotted a postcard on my desk. On the front was a picture of a topless man in a kilt – a rather muscular topless man in a kilt, to be precise. On the back, Joyce had written, '*Having a lovely time, only one dead body so far and lots of beefy men in kilts throwing things around. I might stay, I've yet to find out what they wear underneath. Joyce.*'

Ha, ha, I thought, *wait until she discovers that we really do have a dead body down here, she might regret teasing me like that.* I took my suit jacket off and hung it on the back of the door, then started up my computer. It made a noise not dissimilar to the one I made when I rolled out of bed in the morning; we were both getting on in years, although the computer was easier to fix.

'Ah, you're back.'

I closed my eyes at the sound of Mark's voice. 'I'll never get anything done at this rate.'

'Why change the habit of a lifetime? What did Joe want?'

'To tell us to back off. We were spotted visiting Ralph Jones.'

'So what? We like goats.'

'And gambolling?'

'Err, I guess so.' Mark took a seat in the same location as Joe had occupied. 'I was thinking, I don't have any reason to be back at the museum until we get the all-clear from the police, but it's come to my attention that our eminent director has been invited to an event that's being held right here this evening, so perhaps we should try and have a word with him, get his perspective on recent events. He might be a bit more relaxed away from the museum, and with a glass of wine in his hand...'

'Really? Which one?' I started rifling through a stack of papers on my desk, trying to find the operational order for the event. Had I forgotten something? Was I going to have to conjure catering out of thin air in an afternoon? It wouldn't be the first time. 'Hang on, is that the event up in the Long Gallery? One hundred and fifty people and a talk by a local society of some kind?'

Mark looked at me as if I was a child who needed a little extra care and attention.

'That's the one, dear, and it's a talk by one of the country's most eminent Egyptologists about the significance of the Pilston collection.' I gave a loud sigh of relief. It was an event that was under control. 'Because the ninth Duke funded the dig that features in *my* exhibition,' Mark emphasised the *my* and puffed his chest out, 'the current Duke agreed to host the evening as part of a schedule of related events.'

I thought about what Joe had said. I never set out to beat the police to a conclusion, or to embarrass them, but I couldn't help but want to know more, and people often spoke to me in a way I imagined they would find it hard to do with the police. I didn't know Sheridan Tasker; I'd only met him the once and hadn't learned much about him, but he didn't deserve to end his days wrapped in a sheet in a sarcophagus.

'Okay, let's do it. I'm not working the event, but no one will be surprised if I'm there. I can be checking in, making sure it's all going smoothly.'

'And I have an invitation. So we're all set.'

. . .

The Long Gallery was just that: a narrow wooden-panelled space that was both a gallery and, when it was originally built, a place for people to perambulate when it was raining. Tonight, it was simply laid out with rows of chairs facing a lectern. Next to it, a large photograph of Edward 'Teddy' Fitzwilliam-Scott, the ninth Duke of Ravensbury, had been placed on an easel. The rear of the space had a table of wine glasses and a small team of staff were ready to circulate with canapés.

The walls were lined with portraits of the Fitzwilliam-Scott ancestors, who never looked pleased to have their space invaded by the noise of events such as this. They weren't the most attractive bunch, but fortunately the more recent generations of the family had picked up some good-looking genes along the way. The guests had started to arrive and were being greeted by the current Duke and Elliot Knight. Sheridan Tasker's absence was palpable as the first words out of everyone's mouths were about his death, as they shook the hands of the two men. It was feeling a bit more like a wake rather than the celebration of a man who had funded some incredibly important archaeological digs a couple of generations ago. But that was hardly a surprise.

It was also not unexpected when, in his welcome speech, the Duke announced that the new museum learning space would be named The Sheridan Tasker Education Centre. His words were welcomed with a rapturous round of applause, a few 'hear hears' and glasses raised in the air. A successful evening was almost guaranteed at this point. Elliot Knight sat on the front row, applauding politely as the speaker was welcomed, and I settled myself on a wide window ledge at the back of the room. Mark had opted to stay with me rather than take a seat.

We heard how Teddy made his contribution to the furthering of our understanding of ancient civilisations by doling out large sums of money. By the end of the talk, I had an image of an enthusiastic if lazy man, who wanted to enjoy all the good things in life and was happy to pay others to pursue their dreams. Of course, heading overseas and plundering other countries of their history, then returning to England with trucks full of valuable items we had no right to was more than questionable.

More wine followed the talk and Mark left me to go and mingle. On the grand scale of things, he was a pretty small-fry local celebrity, but that combined with his charm, humour, height and rather eye-catching style meant people were drawn to him. Elliot Knight seemed equally able to turn on the charm and there was little sign of the bumbling academic that I had glimpsed when first meeting him.

Eventually, I spotted the two men together. Mark looked up, caught my eye and pulled an odd expression. I smiled back, hoping he was alright, and opened another bottle of wine, passing it to a member of staff to circulate with. When I looked up again, Mark repeated the same pained expression. Was he unwell?

No, I realised, he wanted me to join them.

15

'Elliot, you remember Sophie? She was the one who first found Sheridan.'

A pained expression crossed Elliot's face.

'Yes, of course, how dreadful. I am sorry, so very sorry. Just awful for you, I hope you've recovered.' Recovery from that sort of thing could take years, but fortunately, I was okay. Plus, it wasn't my first dead body.

'I'm fine, thank you. It must be a very stressful time for you, so much happening – the renovation, a new building and losing someone so key to the project.'

'Yes, yes indeed. It's hard to know where to start, really. Fortunately, everyone involved in the project has been very understanding and no one has complained at the short pause we've put on things. Out of respect, of course, and to allow people to... well, remember and take their time before moving forward.'

'Were you close to Sheridan?'

'I was, or at least I like to think so. We'd known each other for years. He was a regular on many committees and at fundraising events in the area, so I knew him before he became involved with the museum. He was very generous, with both his time and money.'

'Was he crucial to the museum renovation?'

'Absolutely, it wouldn't be happening without him. What he had achieved was remarkable, quite remarkable.' Elliot's wine glass was empty, and I waved over a server who topped us all up.

'It makes it all the more confusing,' I said between sips of wine, 'that someone would want to hurt him, unless it was a case of mistaken identity. Can you think of anyone who disliked him or the work he was doing?'

Elliot didn't hesitate. 'Absolutely not. As far as I'm aware, he was highly respected. This has all come as a huge shock.'

'What about the renovation? Was there any resistance to that and a chance that Sheridan was killed because he was so key to making it happen?'

Elliot shook his head. 'There was some concern early on from the community that we would be destroying the atmosphere and historic feel of the building, but once the plans were released, it was possible for people to see that we were very respectful of the original building and spaces. So there were low-level grumbles amongst the local community, yes, but no more than that.'

'What about his other work, his biscuit company? Did he ever talk about previous disagreements which might have followed him?' asked Mark, leaving Elliot in thought for a moment before he shook his head again.

'We didn't really talk about subjects beyond the museum. I'm afraid I'm not one for small talk.' He laughed a little nervously. 'Give me an old pot or fossil and I'm quite certain I can bore you for hours. Ask me to make idle conversation and I come rather unstuck. It's always been that way.'

That was a level of self-knowledge I didn't often come across. I was disappointed, if that's the right word. I was hoping there would be a campaign against the museum project, or that Sheridan would have mentioned previous hostility in his career, but there was nothing.

'Elliot, terribly sorry to interrupt.' The Duke nodded briefly at Mark and me. 'I have someone I'd like you to meet.' Elliot turned away without another word and left Mark and me drinking our wine in the corner of the room.

'Should we call it a night?' I asked. The crowd was starting to thin out and I doubted we would be missed, especially as I wasn't even invited in the first place.

'We may as well. I've shaken so many hands, I'm going to end up with a repetitive strain injury.'

We took our time. Mark went back to his office to collect a few things, and I chatted to the supervisor who was looking after the serving staff. Another forty-five minutes had passed before we reached the security gate. Elliot was standing on the other side looking at his watch.

'Everything alright?' I asked. 'Do you need a lift anywhere?'

'No, no, thank you. I'm waiting for a taxi. I left my car at the museum, so I'm returning to collect it.'

'Okay, well, goodnight,' I said as we walked away. 'What do you make of Elliot?' I asked Mark once we were out of earshot.

'Hmmm.' There was a long gap as Mark thought about my question. 'I've always rather liked him. He can be a bit absent-minded and gets very lost in his academic work. I can't say that I see him as a natural manager, but that's not necessarily what gets you that kind of job. He's a very good face of the museum, brilliant at raising money.'

'Did you ever get a sense that he didn't get on with Sheridan?'

'No, not once. I didn't see them together very often, but they seemed to get on perfectly well, and when I saw them individually, they only said complimentary things about the other.'

There was nothing more to say at that point, so we hugged and said our goodnights. I had a cat waiting at home for me, and she was no doubt feeling neglected.

I was right. Pumpkin yowled at me with a scolding tone the moment I stepped through the door.

'It's been a day, just one working day. You probably spent most of it sleeping anyway.' Whilst I sorted myself out, Pumpkin kept her distance and scowled at me. She was rather on the large side and when she eventually forgave me and head-butted my leg, I almost lost my footing.

'Pumpkin, you'll leave a bruise.' She head-butted me again. I scratched the top of her head with one hand whilst reaching for her treats with another. 'I'm going to get a lecture at the vet's for overfeeding you, I know I am.'

After a quick shower, I settled under my duvet. Pumpkin walked on top of me until we were nose to nose, and then lay down, at which point she commenced cleaning all the bits I had apparently missed.

'OW, that hurts. I know I washed my face... leave my eyebrow alone.' I tried to close my eyes and ignore her, but it didn't work, so I kissed the top of her head and enjoyed our moment.

I was just about ready to drift off to sleep when my phone rang. Pumpkin leapt off me, her entire body weight pressing into two small paw-sized areas on my chest as she jumped into the air, did a single bounce on the bed, and then shot out of the door. A picture of Mark's face was on the screen.

'This better be good, me and Pump were just doing a little loving.'

'Eugh, please don't tell me any more.'

I closed my eyes. There was no point rolling them, the action would be wasted over the phone.

'So,' he often started a call like he was about to tell a story on one of his tours, 'I arrived home and Joe was here having a beer with Bill. I had just removed the cap from a bottle of rather nice local dark ale…'

'Get on with it.'

'I am! I had barely opened my drink when Joe's phone rang and he had to head off, but not before he told me that there had been an incident at the museum. It appears that Elliot's car has been damaged, intentionally.'

'Having a detective as a brother-in-law *can* have its uses. I'm surprised he told you what had happened.'

'He did give me one of those stares as he left.'

'What kind of stare?'

'Oh, you know, we get them all the time. *I didn't mean to say that out loud and we both know you heard it, but if anyone asks, you didn't, and by the way, if you tell anyone else, especially that Sophie – slash Mark – slash Joyce – there'll be hell to pay.* Of course, hell never does come paying, but at least he can say he warned us. Talking of hell and occupants thereof, I got a postcard off Joyce today, picture of a Highland cow. Apparently I could learn a lot from its facial hair. She's living it up with the lairds of bonnie, bonnie Scotland, but has yet to find out what they wear under their kilt.'

'I got one as well. I wonder how much research she's doing.'

'I have no idea and I'm not going to be the one to ask. Are we meeting at the museum in the morning, try and find out more about this incident?'

'If Pumpkin allows me.' She had made her way back up onto the bed and was lying on my chest again. 'I might have a bad case of feline paralysis.'

'A bad case of what?'

'It's a condition whereby a person is unable to move due to the presence of a cat somewhere on their body.'

'Ah, well I wouldn't put it past that sandbag to give you something far more serious, she's a menace to society.'

'No, she's a menace to you and your delicate disposition. Go to sleep, I'll see you at the museum at nine.' I hung up. 'Right, cat, I'm clean, I'm going to sleep, and you can do the same.'

I could have sworn the look in Pumpkin's eyes translated to *I love your optimism.*

16

I was starting to feel as if I worked at the museum, I spent so much time there, or at the very least that it was an outpost of Charleton House. I knew that all the cafés I was responsible for were in safe hands when I was away, but I was aware that I might be pushing it a bit at the moment. As soon as Mark and I had found out more about the attack on Elliot's car, I would be straight back and would throw myself into being extremely hands-on for the rest of the day. I was going to be a demon barista.

On arriving at the museum, I ran into a familiar-looking security guard. I'd seen him around most of the days that I'd been here. He was an older man with a slim face and wispy grey hair sticking out from under his peaked hat.

I read his name badge. 'Hi… Ian. I'm looking for Mark Boxer, have you seen him?'

'Sure have, he was heading towards the basement first thing. Are you Sophie?'

'I am.'

'Thought so. Hope you're doing alright after the other day. That must have been a mighty shock.'

I smiled. 'I'm okay, thank you.' I was going to take this opportunity. 'Were you working last night?'

'I was. Finished about eleven, then had an early start this morning. One of the lads is on holiday so I said I'd do a couple of his hours.' He grinned. 'Nothing an extra cup of coffee can't help with.'

I laughed. 'I'm the same. Some days it's the only thing that keeps me upright.' Ian gave a little chortle. 'I heard that there was an incident with the director's car. You must have been here when that happened.'

The smile left his face and he looked worried. He nodded.

'Awful. Elliot was understandably upset. He'd got back from some event and he found his car had a bloody big scratch all along the side. Police reckon it was a key what was used. Did a lot of damage.'

'Wasn't it caught on camera?'

'No. He parked off to the side of the car park, right by the trees, where the staff park. The camera doesn't reach over there. He says the spaces closest to the building should be left free for the visitors. I agree with him.'

'Did the cameras not even catch the suspect walking away?'

'Nope. Nothin'. I don't see how the police are going to solve this one.'

'Do they think it might have something to do with the murder?'

Ian shrugged. 'If they do, they ain't telling me, and anyway, we often get kids hanging round the carpark at night, so it could just as easily have been them.'

I was suddenly jolted sideways as someone walked into me.

'Sorry, sorry. My fault.' The woman in the housekeepers' uniform of black cargo pants and a grey polo neck t-shirt looked genuinely apologetic.

'What's up, Dar? You don't look too happy,' said Ian. She flapped the piece of paper she was carrying in the air.

'I don't know how I'm going to get the schedule covered. I've got two on holiday, two off sick and Danny still hasn't turned up, and no one knows where he is. He's not answering his phone either.'

'Danny Jones? That's not like him, he's a reliable chap.'

'Aye, never had a problem with him, and now he just ups sticks.'

'When was the last time he worked?' I asked. Dar looked down at the sheet of paper.

'Day the reception was meant to be taking place. He was doing the night shift that week, but he stepped up to oversee the team that day so I could come in late. I was going to stay around for the reception, and then help with the clean-up at the end of the night. Didn't want to leave too much for the day shift to do the following morning.'

So, we had a member of staff who disappeared around the time of the murder and the theft, with the same surname as the man who had found the coins. That seemed like too much of a coincidence for comfort.

'You realise this puts Elliot out of the frame?'

'I didn't realise he was in it,' replied Mark as he slid a packet of Jaffa Cakes across the table towards me. The police had finished with the gallery, so the museum was able to plan the second attempt to open the exhibition. We were in Mark's windowless office in the basement. The fact that it was a Saturday didn't put him off wanting to get stuck in, and I knew Bill, an ex-pro rugby player who was on his second career as a history teacher, was away at a match with his school.

'He had to be a possibility. Maybe there's someone who is against the project and is warning him off. *Drop the plans or you'll be next.*'

Mark grunted what sounded like an agreement through a mouthful of biscuit.

'And the coins? What's the link there?'

'That's another angle we can take. There's a strong chance that the killer was disturbed stealing the coins and lashed out. Sheridan's death was unplanned and he hadn't actually been an intended target. Wrong place, wrong time sort of thing. You know, one of the cleaners is currently missing. He vanished just before the reception was due to take place and hasn't been seen since.'

That made Mark stop chewing. 'Tell me more,' he spluttered. I told him what I'd learnt from Dar, the housekeeper.

'And what do you notice?'

Mark stared at me, his hand slowly reaching forward for another Jaffa Cake. I slapped it out of the way and took one for myself. He gave my question a nanosecond's thought, and then gave up with a shrug.

'Jones, Danny Jones. I know it's a common surname, but might he be related to Ralph Jones and therefore have a link with the coins?'

Mark sat up straight at that. 'Ooh, nice one, Sophie.' Quick as a flash, he grabbed a Jaffa Cake. 'I think another visit to the farm might be in order, after we've checked that it's the same family. Ralph might not have told us everything.'

'Look, I need to get back to the house, I've been away from the café too much this week. Why don't you try and have a catch up with Elliot, see what he can tell you about last night and if he has any suspicions about who it might have been?'

He gave me a mock salute as his mouth was still full, then swallowed.

'Orders received and understood, and whilst I'm risking the wrath of our trusty constabulary and, in my case, a very awkward dinner the next time the family gets together, what are you going to be up to?'

'I'm going to be saving the world one cup of coffee at a time. That, and trying to keep my staff sweet, which is much more risky than anything you're going to be doing.'

'Agreed, good luck.'

He popped yet another Jaffa Cake into his mouth and I left him to it, but not before I'd grabbed the rest of the packet. Mark emitted a mumbled growl.

17

It turned out I really was a demon barista, as I took a break from emails and anything involving management decisions whilst I helped Chelsea serve a couple of busloads of international visitors. It's amazing how much about food can be communicated via entirely made-up sign language. There was much laughter interspersed with serving the lattes and cakes.

'That's the last of the fruit tarts,' I called out to Tina as she walked from the kitchen.

'Noted. Speaking of which, when is Joyce back? I never thought I'd say this, but I miss her.'

'Do I need to check your temperature?'

'To be more precise, I miss her coming in here and putting you in your place. It's always good entertainment.'

'Thanks, I'm glad I'm good for something. You'll be pleased to hear that she returns on Tuesday. Late, though, so you'll have to wait another day to see her strut her way into the café and make up for lost time with her jokes about my wardrobe or hair.'

'And wanting the latest on Ryan, unless you've been updating her?'

'There's nothing to update her with. He's still on tour and we're currently playing phone tag.'

'Well, something better happen in the next few days, otherwise Joyce is going to be very cross.' Tina wagged her finger at me. 'Knowing her, she'll force the issue and speak to him herself. She'll have you engaged before the end of the week.'

'Don't joke about it.'

'Fine, but I'm not kidding.' I knew she wasn't, so I decided that calling Ryan would be close to the top of my to-do list later today. Besides which, I had decided that he could be a good person to talk to about the coin theft from the museum. He might be able to give me some background on that sort of thing.

'Sophie, good afternoon.' The sound of the Duke's voice brought me out of my thoughts.

'Good afternoon. What can I get for you?' I could see a few heads turn, out of the corner of my eye. Visitors were always surprised to see the Duke and Duchess walking around. They imagined the closest they would get to them would be the photographs on the inside of the guides, but apart from the fact that the Duke and Duchess took the visitor engagement side of their work very seriously, Charleton House was their family home and they didn't always want to be limited to the areas that were out of bounds to the public. If I was them, I'd be overjoyed to have a café – make that multiple cafés – in my own house, so the visitors would see a lot of me, no matter what I thought of them.

'Nothing, thank you, I was just passing. Have you heard anything more about events at the museum? You usually have your ear to the ground.'

I shook my head. 'Did you have the opportunity to visit Sheridan's mother?' I asked.

'I did. Of course, she'd had the police there that morning and I couldn't tell her anything she didn't already know, but I think she appreciated my going around to see her. She was still in shock.

Her daughter arrived before I left, so I know she is in good hands.'

I stepped away from the counter and gave Chelsea a look which she correctly interpreted as *please take over*. The Duke moved with me, and although he didn't show any signs of wanting to sit, we did at least have a little more privacy. I was still cautious about letting on just how interested I was in the case. Things were certainly starting to thaw between me and the Duke and Duchess after a case I ended up involved with resulted in their younger son going to prison, but I didn't want to push my luck.

'I haven't heard any more about the murder investigation, but there was an act of vandalism last night. Elliot's car was keyed.'

'His car was *what*?'

'Keyed. Someone scratched a key, or some other sharp object, along the side of his car.'

The Duke tutted. 'What has the world come to? They really haven't had much luck at the Pilston. Deaths, thefts, and vandals.'

I wouldn't have ordinarily interrupted the Duke of Ravensbury as he spoke, but I couldn't let that go.

'Deaths and thefts? So there has been a previous murder, and more thefts?'

'Oh, not a murder, no, no.' The Duke appeared to relax a little, as though discussing something other than his friend's demise was a relief, even if the subject was someone else's demise. 'It was a heart attack whilst at work, a curator. He was an older man, died at his desk. Apparently he was a workaholic and it was what he would have wanted.'

'And the thefts?'

'Oh, what museum hasn't had thefts? The Pilston has been very unfortunate, though. Over the years, they've had everything go missing from rugs and vases to fossils, and even, I believe, a snail.'

'A snail?'

'Yes. A particularly rare and beautiful snail. The shell was something to behold.'

'And they never found the people who did it?'

'No, I'm afraid not. It's gone on for many years. I must be going. Don't want to hold you up.'

And with that he turned, and with long strides left the café.

'Sophie.'

'Hmm?'

'Phone call, in your office. A certain historian.'

Ryan? I couldn't remember the last time I'd run towards the office so quickly; it was more common for me to run out of it. I stopped briefly to check my hair in the reflection on the kitchen windows, then remembered he was on the phone and I was an idiot.

'Ryan,' I said, a little too breathlessly to be cool as I landed in my seat and picked up the phone simultaneously.

'Hello, stranger.' He laughed nervously. 'I've been trying to get hold of you.'

'I know, sorry about that. I left you a message.'

'I got it, thank you. I heard about events at the Pilston and I know Mark has been working there. How is he?'

So, he didn't know I'd found the body. I filled him in on what had happened and was left with silence on the end of the line.

'Are you still there?'

'Yes, but a little in shock. How come you sound so calm about it all? You found a dead body.'

'It's not the first time.'

'It's not the... what?'

'Nothing dramatic.' A lie, but this wasn't the time to start discussing my proclivity for discovering the dead. 'Look, I was wondering, have you had much to do with the Pilston? Do you know much about the place?'

'A little. Why?'

'Mark's working there, someone dies there. I'm just curious to know more. You're a historian, you must feel the same way about things that capture your interest.'

He laughed, which resulted in me smiling like a loon.

'Yes, I admit, I do spend a lot of time going down rabbit holes in my line of work, and often they can be quite revealing rabbit holes.' There was a lightness in his voice which convinced me that I had distracted him from the shocking revelation of my connection to the body. 'To a large extent, it's your typical local country museum, only with a rather important collection. It certainly doesn't have the number of visitors it deserves, but I imagine the refurbishment and additional building are part of trying to resolve that.'

'Has it been involved in any scandals? Anything that might not have made the news?'

'You mean like more bodies turning up?' Okay, so he hadn't been distracted that much.

'Or thefts, I heard they've had quite a lot of those.'

'They have, and they've never been able to catch who did it. There has always been a lot of talk about many of them being inside jobs, but like most museums their size, the Pilston's security isn't the best and it probably wouldn't be hard for someone who knew what they were doing to break in.'

'Was it always a similar kind of object stolen?'

There was silence on the other end and I wondered if I'd lost him, or bored him, but he quickly returned.

'I'm trying to remember the various thefts, but I'm struggling. I can't think of anything that stands out.'

'Which means there probably wasn't a pattern.'

'I guess so. Sorry, Sophie, I'm going to have to go. My publicist is waving at me, our car has arrived. I'm glad we finally got to catch up, though. Maybe I can call again when we get to our next hotel, or...'

'I'd like that.'

'Great.' And he really did sound excited. 'Bye.' He hung up before I had a chance to say my own farewell.

'Are you sure he's not gay?'

I spun round in my chair. Tina was leaning against the doorframe.

'What?'

'Well, that just sounded like one of the many conversations you have with Mark when you've got your nose stuck into something dark and mysterious. You weren't exactly whispering sweet nothings.'

'I've known him for five minutes. It's early days, and anyway, he might have been able to help with the current dark and mysterious goings-on in my life. And no, he's not gay.'

'How do you know? Ooooh, Sophie, have you…?'

'No, we have not, and I'd hardly tell you if we had. A goodnight kiss is as far as it's got.'

'What kind of kiss?'

'Get out, or I'll fire you.'

Tina grinned and slunk away from the door. 'I'll be able to tell, you know, if you two…' she called over her shoulder. I threw a squishy purple stress ball out of the door. It went nowhere near her and ended up in a bowl of salad.

18

'I asked him if he thought he was the intended target of the killer and he dismissed it without hesitation.'

Mark was enjoying a pint of local ale after a long day at the museum and filling me in on his conversation with Elliot.

'How's the gin? I guessed what you'd want.'

'Good. He's really not worried?'

Mark was looking across the pub, then seemed to realise I'd spoken and turned to face me. 'Hmm? Oh, well I wouldn't say not worried. He's obviously worried about everything that's going on, but he doesn't seem to think that he's at risk.' Then he was back to looking across the room.

'What about the coins? Does he have any theories about the coins?'

'I forgot to ask him, but I did find out something very interesting about that. Danny Jones is indeed the son of Ralph Jones. Not only that, but when the coins were found, Danny was very vocal about keeping them in the family. He was only fifteen at the time, but still...'

'He could have been planning on getting them back all this time, finally got round to it, and when he did steal them, he ran into Sheridan, panicked, killed him and stuffed him in the sarcophagus in the hope it would take a while for someone to find his body.'

'We were about to put it on display, it wasn't going to take long for someone to find Sheridan. At the very latest, we'd have found him later that day when the sarcophagus was lifted into position.'

I thought about that. 'He panicked, then. But as we've discussed before, it's a bit of a coincidence that Sheridan was found inside a sarcophagus that he had petitioned to have in the exhibition, which suggests that someone knew him well enough to know that it was important to him. Perhaps they were making a statement. How would Danny know about that?'

'It would have been easy enough for him to overhear multiple conversations about the exhibition. We've had a lot of meetings and discussions out in the galleries, and Sheridan joined in some of those. We weren't trying to keep it a secret, plus I'm sure that Sheridan mentioned his love of Egyptology in interviews.'

'We should go to the farm again, try and find Danny. He might have told his father where he is, but he also might be hiding from everyone right now. His father was keen to donate the coins, so he's hardly going to be supportive of what his son has done, or might have done. But if he does know where Danny is, then Ralph is a very good actor.'

There was silence.

'Mark?'

No answer.

'Oi. Hello, Earth calling Mark. What's so interesting?' I tried to see who or what Mark was staring at, but the Black Swan pub was busy with a noisy Saturday evening crowd.

'I recognise him, I'm sure I do. The man in the blue t-shirt.' The man in question could only be described as average. Average height, average weight, mousy brown hair that hadn't been cut in what might be considered a particular style. His jeans didn't fit him very well and he wore tired-looking brown shoes.

'I'm not surprised you're struggling to place him. I've never seen such a bland-looking man.'

'Got it! He works at the museum. I was talking to Elliot when that bloke started walking down the corridor. Elliot practically dragged me into the nearest room to avoid talking to him. Says he's a major pain in the neck, complains about everything.'

'Kit!' I declared. 'That has to be Kit Porter, he even looks quite like his sister.'

'You know him?'

'I know of him. He started a petition against the renovation. Didn't get far with it, but if he's dead set against the renovation, then he has a motive to get rid of Sheridan. Come on, I feel the need to stand up, get a bit closer to the lively atmosphere at the bar.'

I grabbed my glass and walked over to where Kit was standing waiting to get served. Pretending not to see him, I looked around, taking in the wooden beams with their glinting horse brasses. It was a lovely old pub, quaint and full of locals who recognised one another, as well as a deluge of tourists in the summer months.

Eventually, I settled my eyes on him.

'Oh, hello,' I said, trying to sound surprised. 'Aren't you... don't I know you? I'm so sorry, but you are very familiar, have we met before?'

Kit stared at me. 'I don't think so.'

'Hang on, have you got a sister? Sharon?'

'Yes.' He sounded wary, and looked hesitant to give away too much.

'Sharon Porter, of course, you look very alike. I work with her at Charleton House. She's such a dedicated member of staff, the Duke and Duchess are very lucky to have her.'

With that, he seemed to relax. 'My sister's a very hard worker. And you are?'

'Sophie Lockwood, I run the cafés, and this is Mark Boxer, a tour guide.'

Kit shook our hands. 'Yes, I know you, Mark. You're putting together the exhibition about the duke and the lord.' He still had a slightly wary look in his eyes, but he did give the impression of being up for a conversation.

'It's horrifying, what happened at the museum,' I said, knowing that it was unlikely anyone would start a conversation with Kit about anything else but the murder once they knew where he worked, so diving straight in with it was fine.

'Indeed. I've been working with management to make sure that all staff have access to counselling, should they need it, and I've requested a presentation be delivered about the security provisions in place, and what new procedures will be instated to ensure everyone's safety. As I'm sure you can imagine, there are a lot of very nervous staff now, wondering who might be next.' That all sounded reasonable. 'I've drawn up a security plan, laid out the need for additional staff, asked for martial arts training for us all, and requested that pepper spray be ordered for all staff to carry.' Okay, so that went a bit far, and as pepper spray is illegal in the UK, he'd have a problem with that part of his plan.

'I bet the security team were overjoyed to receive all of those proposals,' Mark replied, the sarcasm a little too apparent.

'So, you think that Sheridan was just a random target?' I asked, trying to take Kit's attention away from Mark.

'I didn't say that, but you can understand the feelings of those who are concerned.'

'Oh, of course, I can absolutely understand. I'm sure it makes the museum a very challenging place to be right now.' My gin was getting low and I tried glancing at Mark, but he didn't get the hint.

'What is it like to work at the museum full time?' asked Mark, doing his best to sound nonchalant. 'I'm only skirting around the edges of life there, so to speak, so I'm curious if it might be somewhere I should be aspiring to be involved in further projects.'

'It has one of the finest collections in the country, why wouldn't you want to work there?' said Kit, sounding rather defensive.

'Oh, you know, somewhere can look rather good from the outside, but on the inside, it's all scandal and backbiting and management don't really have a good grasp of things. Those sorts of places tend to do so well because of the passion of people like yourself.'

Good man, Mark, butter him up, I thought. *Works better than sarcastic digs.*

Kit was staring into his pint glass, apparently deep in thought. 'As I said before, anyone should be proud to work at the Pilston, but yes, there are a few of us who are doing our best to keep the place moving in the right direction, and it is rather an uphill battle.'

'Do you mean the renovation?' I asked. 'I'm sure that not everyone was keen on that project.'

Kit looked at the heavens in disbelief. 'Can you blame us? I assume they were seeking some kind of architectural award when they chose the final design. There is absolutely nothing wrong with the museum as it stands. Yes, it needs some care and attention, and that is where the money should be going. Not on some glorified tin can stuck on the side of the building. We are not Bilbao, we are not the Louvre, we are not the Pompidou. Were our views taken into account, though? Of course not.'

I half expected to see steam coming out of his ears.

'I believe that Elliot and Sheridan have been quite the duo, working on this. Did they not listen to staff input?'

'There were a few forums held, and a suggestion box, but it wasn't enough.'

It didn't result in you getting what you wanted, is what you really mean, I thought.

'Shocking,' said Mark, sounding not very shocked at all. 'I would have got a petition going, or led a strike.'

'I did. Well, not a strike, but I circulated a petition.'

'You clearly worked really hard to try and get the build stopped, and I suppose now it is, or paused at least. This will give you the opportunity to try again. The fight must go on.' It was easy for me to tell that Mark wasn't keen on Kit and he was trying his hardest to rein himself in, which wasn't very hard at all.

'Mark, could you get me a gin and tonic? Get Kit here another drink while you're at it.'

Kit handed over his empty glass without saying a word and Mark wandered off to the bar, looking confused and giving me a questioning glance. I chatted for a little while with Kit about how long he had worked at the museum – over thirty years – how much it had changed, what he loved about the place. It was clear that he was passionate, and overbearing and annoying as hell, but would all of that spill over into killing someone?

'I know many would say that I am stuck in the past, that I am treating the museum like a mausoleum, but that's not entirely a bad thing, is it?' He wasn't expecting me to answer. He was looking over my shoulder at some imaginary status quo, a hard expression on his face. 'The museum is in a unique position to tell us about fascinating aspects of the world's history, human and natural, and it does that perfectly well in its current form.'

'But can't that be done in a sympathetically renovated building and an extension?'

'No,' he said firmly. 'No, it cannot. It will change everything about the place and that cannot happen.'

'Wow!' said Mark dramatically after we had left Kit with his fresh pint and found a table next to the fireplace. 'There's a man who knows his mind.'

'There's a man who's terrified of change,' I added.

'In an almost pathological way. I don't think he'd let much get in the way of his plans for the museum, or rather his lack of plans. As soon as all reasonable paths to fight the work are closed off to him, one of the main movers and shakers in the project turns up dead. A coincidence? I think not,' he said with a comically knowing look on his face.

'I don't know. Every workplace has their Kit. We have his sister Sharon for a start. They'll argue against anything almost for the sake of it – they're not happy unless they're in the middle of a battle. Sharon spent six months complaining because the ticket office staff were given new uniform shirts and the collar shape was different to the last one. I thought she was going to use one of the new shirts to murder the entire HR team. Kit must be very annoying to have to manage – or work with at all, frankly – but I just don't think he's a killer.'

'That's a shame. At this rate, the murder will remain unsolved and the exhibition is going to pass by almost unnoticed.'

'Oh no, a man's death is going to pull publicity away from your little project. How awful.'

'Indeed, it's unacceptable,' he grumbled as he buried his face in his pint. 'Oh hell.' He sat up and turned in his chair so he was sideways to the table. A woman on the other side of the fireplace had spotted him and was taking photos. 'Someone kill me now. Sorry, unfortunate turn of phrase.'

'What's wrong? You don't typically mind when someone recognises you.'

'I know, but I was distracted this morning and my socks don't match my tie.'

'Are you serious?'

'Of course.' He looked confused that I'd question such a thing.

'Okay then, that's definitely a reason to seek your own demise.'

19

'Let me look.' I peered under the picnic table at Mark's feet. The gravel crunched as he shuffled them.

'What are you doing?'

'After last night's comment, I'm just checking that you matched your socks with your tie this morning and I don't need to start planning your funeral.'

'Very funny, not. Look, I think you might be right…'

'Sorry, can you say that again? You think I might be what? What am I?'

Mark screwed up his eyes and I smirked.

'I'm not saying it again.' He took a sip of coffee, and then continued, 'I'm doubtful about Kit being involved. Deeply irritating, yes, but a killer, no.'

'Oh, I don't know, he's got that killer's look about him.'

We did a synchronised head-turn to look at Mimi, who was clearing the table next to ours.

'Sorry, I couldn't help overhearing, and that was rather flippant of me, but still, I find him a deeply questionable individual and I have sometimes wondered what lengths he'd go to in order to win one of his *issues*.' She said the last word with a distinctly mocking tone. 'I always thought he was the one who made that voodoo doll of Elliot. Some said it was the curse, but I don't believe in any of that.'

'Mimi, put those plates down and come and join us, just for a minute. There isn't a queue.' Mark moved along the bench so that she could sit next to him. She held her skirt in one hand so she maintained some semblance of dignity as she climbed over. 'Can you just go over that again? A voodoo doll, you said?'

'Horrible, it was. It looked just like Elliot, same glasses, same tweed jacket. It had little pins stuck all over it.'

'Where was it found?' I asked.

'It arrived in a box, in the mail. The postie dropped it off at the main information desk because the museum was open. There was a local postmark on it, but no return address.'

'No fingerprints?'

'Oh no, Elliot never bothered with any of that, didn't tell the police. He said it wasn't worth it, that it was a stupid joke.'

'Why do you think it was Kit? It could have been anyone, and not necessarily a member of staff.' Mark nodded as I spoke.

'It was just the way he behaved. He was there when it was opened, and so was I – I was waiting for a parcel and had seen the post van arrive. Well, Kit's response just seemed so unnatural, staged. He said all the right things – *"Oh, how awful... that's shocking... no one deserves something like this..."* but it wasn't heartfelt. It was like he was reading from a script. Then he went about his business. Ordinarily, he'd have blown up at something like that. Insisted on investigations, gone on about unhealthy work environments and cultures of fear, but not this time. He just slunk off and didn't say a lot more about it. It wasn't normal for him.'

'How long ago did this happen?'

'Last month, I reckon. Yes, that's right, I was waiting for my delivery of new aprons.' She leaned back so we could see the front of her pale blue apron. It had an illustration of one of the sabre-toothed tigers from inside the museum and the words *'Fancy a bite?'* and made me wonder if I needed to get a bit more imaginative with the uniforms of my own staff. I wasn't sure the Duke and Duchess would be so keen on aprons that said things like *'You mocha me very happy'* or *'Thanks a latte'*.

'Have the police been told now, since the murder?' Mark asked.

'I haven't a clue. I better go, I can see people heading this way. They'll be wanting a drink, I'm sure.' Mimi climbed over the bench and gave a cheery, 'I'm on my way,' to the customers who were starting to line up at the window of the horsebox.

'We should talk to Joe. If the police don't know about the doll, then we might get credit for passing the information on rather than being accused of not telling them stuff.'

'Which, if we're honest, is usually true,' Mark reminded me.

'Sometimes, not always. Tell me about the curse she mentioned.'

'Usual ridiculous thing. Remember the curse of King Tut?' I nodded. Nine people who had been involved in the discovery of Tutankhamun's tomb had later died, and some had attributed it to a curse placed on them when they disturbed the king's resting place. 'It's a bit like that. Multiple thefts, a few injuries, one heart attack. They were all the kinds of things that could happen anywhere, but some like to say they were the result of a curse. What or who put that curse on the museum staff isn't clear.'

'Have you heard of any rumours circulating about it amongst the staff since you've been here?'

'Why, do you believe it?' He sounded incredulous.

'No, but it could be a pattern of intimidation designed to mislead the police.'

'But some of the events happened years ago.'

'True, but if the killer could get people talking, try and tie all the recent events in with rumours about the curse, it might serve as a useful distraction.'

As I spoke, I actually found myself convinced by the seemingly outlandish idea. Quite how I was going to raise it with Joe, I had no clue.

20

'A voodoo doll? Are you serious?'

'Quite serious. Even if we think the whole notion of voodoo dolls and curses is ridiculous, it's not beyond the wit of someone to use it as a cover and for others to be genuinely afraid.'

'So, you think this voodoo doll is related to Sheridan's murder?' Joe bit the head off a gingerbread man I had given him and gave me a cocky sneer. 'A leg next, I reckon,' he muttered. 'Or maybe you've got a toothpick I can stick in its heart.'

'You're meant to take the concerns of the community seriously, no matter how outlandish. I have no idea how the community is going to take you seriously with crumbs all down your front, though.'

He put the gingerbread man down and started brushing himself with his hands. 'We'll talk to Elliot about it,' he said. 'Hopefully he's still got the doll and we can send it off to the lab, there might be something useful on it. I imagine it's too much to hope that he kept hold of the packaging.'

'You know what this means?'

'Go on, enlighten me, Miss Marple.'

'It means that there is a strong chance that Sheridan wasn't the intended target.'

'You're on fire today.'

I threw my hands into the air. 'What have I done wrong? I'm helping you with your inquiries.'

'Sorry. Harnby is still in a mood and I have no idea why. All I know is I'm getting the brunt of it. And I forgot I was meant to be taking Ellie out for dinner last night and left her sitting in a restaurant while I was still in the office, and Mum got wildly drunk in the pub and made a fool of herself.' I knew that Joe's mum was a bit of a drinker. She could stop for months, and then binge. Joe had never said anything, but I'd always known that he was afraid it would tip over into something more consistent, and serious.

'Okay, you're entitled to be a bit grumpy today. Not about Ellie, though, that's your own daft fault.' He gave me a pained look. 'Sisterhood,' I said, raising a fist. 'Mess one of us about, you have to deal with all of us.'

'Got any ideas how I can make it up to her?'

'I don't know why I should help you, but I'll give you a cake and a coffee to take to her. Call first, though. You wander into the conservation lab scattering crumbs and she'll probably never talk to you again.'

'Good tip.'

I put a strawberry tart in a box and, after managing to find a ribbon in the bottom of a drawer of clutter, attached a bow. I also tied ribbon around the coffee cup I sent him away with.

'Is that a service you offer everyone?' the Duke asked, watching Joe leave.

'His girlfriend is Ellie Bryant in the conservation department, and he needs to make up a few brownie points.'

'Ah yes, I've been in that position on a number of occasions over the years. I wish him luck. Now, talking of gifts and bows, that's exactly what I've come to talk to you about.' I grabbed a notepad and pen. 'I'm off to London and the Duchess is coming with me, but we'd like Harriet Tasker, Sheridan's wife – although I suppose she's his widow now – to know we are thinking about her. Could you put together some sort of gift basket for her? Baked goods, bottle of wine, chocolates, ask the gardeners to create a nice bouquet of flowers? We'll phone while we're away, of course, but I feel the need to do more.'

'Certainly. When would you like it done for?'

'Tomorrow? I'll arrange for someone to deliver it.'

'That's quite alright, I'll take it.'

'Oh heavens, Sophie, are you sure that isn't an imposition?'

If only he knew how much time I spend away from my job, I thought. I'd just been presented with the perfect excuse to visit Sheridan's home and talk to his wife. This was either utterly perfect, or I was about to get myself into a lot of trouble. Well, in for a penny, in for a pound. I wrote down the address and said goodbye to the Duke, questions for Harriet already starting to form in my mind.

'Well, you landed on your investigative feet. What are you hoping to find out?' Mark sounded impressed. It was late and I was lying on the sofa as I spoke to him, the phone wedged between my ear and the pillow.

'I'll probably have to play it by ear, depending on how distraught Harriet is. She might not even invite me in.'

'She might not what?'

'Invite me in.'

'Ask you to do what? Bloody hell, buy a new phone, will you.'

'There's nothing wrong with this phone. I can't put it on speaker, that's all.'

'Which means there is something wrong with it.'

'You heard all that. OW!' Pumpkin was making biscuits on me, her claws sticking in my chest with increasing ferocity. It felt like she was trying to make a point, I just didn't know what that point was. 'Pumpkin's turning me into a pin cushion.'

'You should have her put down.'

'*Mark*! How dare you! I'll have you put down before I let a vet get anywhere near her.'

'I'll do it for you.'

'Can we move on? I'm going to head over mid-morning. I'll return to work via the museum and tell you how it went, assuming you don't make any more disparaging comments about my cat between now and then.'

'What is she doing right now?'

'Umm...' I looked down at where Pumpkin's paws were rhythmically softening me up '...putting holes in my nightshirt. Oi, cat, stop it.' I pushed her off.

'I rest my case.'

'Get some sleep,' I instructed him. 'We need to put our heads together tomorrow because we are getting nowhere. I expect you to be on top form.'

With that, I hung up and looked at my shirt. There were three decent-sized holes. Wretched cat!

21

J had loaded the car with the obscenely decadent gift basket I had put together. I knew the Duke's tastes stretched to the excessive and grandiose, and he was an inherently generous man, so I really had gone to town on the contents. Besides which, the recipient's husband had just been murdered, so she deserved the most expensive chocolates in the gift shop.

I drove carefully up the short driveway to the Taskers' home, my tyres sounding sticky against the perfectly smooth tarmac. The main house was built on a raised area of land. Tucked beneath it at ground level were three large black garage doors, to the left of them a sweeping stone staircase, terracing continuing in front of the house. A glass balcony looked out over the garages, but there was no one watching my arrival, despite my having had to announce my presence via the intercom at the locked gate.

As I climbed the stairs, leaning to one side to counteract the weight of the basket in my opposite hand, the main house was gradually revealed to me. It was a million miles away from Charleton House in style: a large, modern white building, with enormous glass windows that reflected the morning sun and left me squinting. There were neatly pruned shrubs in tubs around the door, and pots of flowers on the balcony.

I was welcomed in by a young woman who looked as if she had been crying.

'Mum's by the pool, I'll take you through.' The plain white entranceway was overlooked by a mezzanine. The vast chandelier above looked like it had been made out of toilet rolls, but I guessed that it wasn't actually a child's school project and was probably a vastly expensive piece of modern art. The kitchen was as spacious and airy as I expected, the eggshell-blue cupboard doors and the chunky wooden furniture giving it a warm cottagey feel. The table was laid for dinner, the crockery more eggshell blue. It looked as if it was set up for a photo shoot, not a family meal. I didn't want to think about what a kitchen like this cost.

Round a corner, I spied a games room, with full-size snooker table and jukebox. I could make out a row of posters, each advertising a different Egyptian exhibition at museums around the world, as I followed Harriet's daughter out through large patio doors and into a garden that would have looked more at home outside a Spanish villa. The area closest to the house held a large turquoise-blue pool. It looked cool and inviting. The day wasn't all that warm, but I still would have happily jumped in. A potted palm tree stood in every corner of the terrace, swaying slightly in the breeze. I was surprised they survived in this part of the world, but I also imagined that they were looked after by a team of professional gardeners who knew what to do with them, and maybe even stored them somewhere warm in the worst of the British winters.

Beside the pool, modern grey wicker chairs surrounded a long matching table with a glass top, and it was here that we found Harriet Tasker. She stood as she saw me, and her daughter went straight back into the house. Harriet was a tall and elegant woman, the simple navy linen shirt and trousers she wore making her look timeless. I found it hard to place her age, and I guessed that she'd had some cosmetic surgery to slow down the onward march of time, but not too much. She didn't have that strained look of a woman who had been pulled taut.

'Please, put it on here.' I placed the basket on the table and she smiled. 'Alexander has always been very thoughtful. Have a seat, can I get you anything to drink?'

'No, thank you.'

She removed the card that had been tucked alongside a block of cheese and read it while still standing.

'Sophie, right?' I nodded. 'Alexander messaged to say you'd be delivering it. Are you sure you won't have a drink?' As she sat, she indicated towards a bottle of rosé in an ice bucket.

'I'm driving, otherwise…' I sounded apologetic that I couldn't indulge, which was unnecessary, and so very English.

'Of course, very wise. I'm afraid I need it to take the edge off.'

'I'm so sorry about your husband.' She acknowledged my words silently. There was a stillness to the entire scene, her movements slow and sorrowful. The tearstained face of the young woman who had shown me through had set the tone and it continued out here.

'It was Shed who wanted the pool included when we built this place. I thought it would end up unused, except for one or two days a year when the British summer was warm enough to make it bearable, but he was in here every day, and we hosted many parties in the garden. It was noisy wherever he went. Not unnecessarily so, he just brought a room to life.'

I was starting to wonder if I would be able to bring myself to quiz a grieving widow, when she seemed to give herself a little shake, took a gulp of wine and turned to face me.

'This isn't what he would have wanted, me wallowing in grief. He'd tell me to swim in the pool, not in tears. So, Sophie, distract me. Tell me what you do for Alexander.'

For the next half an hour, I talked about my job and Harriet asked questions. I was happy to entertain her, and she appeared genuinely interested. Eventually, I took a risk.

'Tell me about Sheridan, if you'd like to.'

Harriet sat back and smiled. 'Most people are afraid to talk about him, in case it upsets me even more. But he's all I want to talk about.' She paused while she topped up her wine glass, holding the bottle in my direction with a single eyebrow raised. I waved away her offer as politely as I could.

'I always thought that it would be a heart attack that got him, he worked so hard. But then in the last couple of years, he began to step away from the business and eventually sold it. Of course, it wasn't long until he filled his time with committees and fundraising events. He wasn't one to sit still for very long.

'I wasn't at all surprised when he told me about the project at the Pilston Museum. He loved that place. He'd gone as a child and he used to take our children there. Every wet weekend, he'd take them in for an hour or two. Becoming chair of the trustees was as much of an achievement for him as the successful running of the business. He'd built two new factories whilst he ran the company, and had this place built, along with the renovation of our house in the Lake District, so he knew a thing or two about working with architects. He was perfect for Pilston.'

'And it was going well?' I asked.

'As far as I know. He always came back very excited. He said a lot would have to change to ensure that the museum met the needs of the 21st century, and that it was bogged down with history, whatever that means. He was even talking about donating more money to the project, it meant so much to him.'

I thought back to the museum. I was certain that the restrictions of building regulations associated with a historic site like Pilston were many and a challenge to navigate. It wouldn't have been an easy project, but there were plenty of architects who specialised in that kind of work, and consultants who could advise them.

'Did he never talk of any difficulties he was facing, or people who were getting in the way of what he had planned?'

She was silent for a little while, then put the wine glass down on the table.

'He didn't often talk about his work, although he always brought me in at the end to celebrate with him. I have my own work, so I was busy too. He did comment once or twice about a couple of *wannabe spanners.*' She formed air quotes with her fingers.

'And the day he died, was there anything unusual?'

She shook her head slowly, looking a little confused. I could tell she was beginning to become uncomfortable with this line of questioning.

'He played golf in the morning, then a business acquaintance came over in the afternoon. He'd had some bad news and wanted to talk it through. Shed said afterwards that there had been a problem, but he was able to fix it and it wouldn't be a long-term issue.'

'There's something I haven't told you.' She looked up at me, but there was only curiosity in her expression. 'I found your husband's body. I was in the gallery early in the morning and, well, he was there.'

She froze for a moment, then softened. 'Did he look like he had suffered?'

I shook my head. 'No, no, he didn't.' It was true. Admittedly, I could only see his face, so I had no idea what condition the rest of him was in, but I wasn't lying.

'They said he would have died quickly, that the knife hit some major arteries and it wouldn't have taken long.'

So, he had been stabbed. All evidence of his injuries was hidden from me in the shadows of the sarcophagus. I hadn't seen anything beyond his neck.

'Did he ever talk about anyone threatening him?' If he didn't talk to her about biscuits, I couldn't imagine him telling her if he was in trouble, but it was worth a try.

She shook her head slowly and sadly, and simply said no.

22

I was walking down the stone staircase to my car when Elliot arrived, the ugly scratch still running along the side of his. It wasn't a fancy car by any means, but it still must have stung when he saw it. If he was surprised to see me, he didn't show it.

'I hope they catch who did it,' I said as I continued to look at the nasty scar in the red paint.

'I don't hold out much hope, it was probably bored kids. I believe there are some who congregate in the car park late at night.' He wore the same tweed jacket I'd seen him in every day so far, and his dark brown trousers had a neat crease running down the legs. He looked tired.

'Do you know Harriet?' he asked.

'No, I was making a delivery on behalf of the Duke.'

'Ah yes, they are friends, I believe. Family connections.' He appeared to be studying me. 'Sophie, isn't it?'

'Yes, Sophie Lockwood.'

'Mark speaks very highly of you. He did suggest we ask you to come and consult as part of the renovation project, as there are plans for a new café. Of course, we'll have to see what happens now.'

'Is there doubt that the project will go ahead?'

'No, no, not at all, at least as far as I know. The project team will need to meet and the trustees will need to discuss it, but we've put far too much work in and this will be Sheridan's legacy.'

He made a move, but I had another question for him. 'The thefts that have happened over the last decade or so, did you develop any theories about them? Did you have any suspects?'

He shook his head. 'The stolen items were so varied, there was no pattern to it, and none ended up being sold, or not that we could find. Why, do you think there might be a connection to Sheridan?'

'The coins went missing right around the time of his death, but I don't know. I just hate to hear about that kind of thing. It seems so pointless if someone is simply going to hide beautiful objects away so no one else can see them.'

He looked at me intently again, and then smiled. 'I can see why Mark enjoys having you around. You have a curious mind.' From anyone else, that could have sounded creepy, but there was something very unthreatening about Elliot. I watched him walk up the steps, wondering again about the coins. Was Harriet hiding something? Maybe there was a link, maybe it was Sheridan who had stolen them, maybe he'd been at the museum to take something else. Mark and I still needed to find Danny Jones. Even if he didn't steal them, he might know something; he worked the late shift on the night of the murder, after all.

There was no escaping the fact that Danny had had access to the gallery alone, that he knew the importance of the coins, that he might have reason to want them back. After all, they had been found on his family's land, and now he had vanished. He was a young man, perhaps he had dreamt of what he could do with the money if he was able to sell them. Maybe he wanted to get away from Derbyshire, head to the bright lights of a city or travel the world.

I left Sheridan and Harriet's house and drove straight to the Jones family farm. Ralph's home was a world away from the Tasker house, a well-kept barn renovation, the farm cottage next door made from limestone that gave off a warm hue in the sunlight, and pretty gardens that, although not perfect, were well loved. Even the patches of mud on the track past the house gave the place a friendly air. None of that harsh, unfeeling concrete with little to soften it.

I buzzed for attention at the gate. There was no sign of anyone. I buzzed again. Eventually, a shaggy-haired youth appeared from one of the barns, an enormous feeding bottle in his hands. He stared at me, and then wandered down the track, in no great hurry.

'Must be a big baby,' I said as he got close, nodding my head towards the bottle in his hands. The joke was lost on him.

'What? Oh, no, we have some calves that need bottle feeding.' He was a strapping lad and had the healthy, tanned look of someone who spent a lot of time outdoors, just like his father, but he was too young to be Danny. He peered at me from behind his long scruffy fringe. If he stood up straight, brushed his hair out of his eyes and smiled, he'd probably be a very good-looking young man.

'I'm looking for your brother, do you know where I'll find him?'

He examined me for a moment. 'No, not seen him for days, dunno where he is.'

'The museum was expecting him at work, maybe you should be worried about him.'

He laughed, although it sounded like the kind of little snort one of the calves might make.

'Danny? God, no, he can take care of 'imself.'

'There must be somewhere he goes when he wants a break. Don't you know where that is?'

'He lives his life, I live mine.' He looked over his shoulder. He didn't seem very at ease, despite all his faux bravado.

'You know there was a murder at the museum, and Danny went missing around the same time. Don't you think that looks suspicious?'

'Danny would never hurt anyone,' he blurted out. There was a faint hint of desperation in those words, of tenderness. The brothers were clearly closer than he was trying to make out.

'He needs to be able to tell the police that. If he wasn't involved, then there'll be no evidence that says otherwise.'

'Who are you anyway? You don't look like police.'

'That's because I'm not. I just want the right person to be arrested and if Danny isn't that person, then the police need to be able to take him off the list of suspects and focus their energies on finding the real killer.'

He stared at me and I felt like I was starting to get through. He glanced over his shoulder again.

'Is he in the barn?'

'No.' There was a clatter, the sound of buckets being kicked over and skidding across a stone floor. Somebody let out a curse. He looked over his shoulder once more. 'You should go, I need to get back to work.'

'*Danny*. Come and talk to me.'

'There's no one here but me, I told you.'

He turned on his heels and walked quickly back up to the open doors of the barn. Bugger this. I wasn't giving up that easily, turned away by someone who was essentially still a boy.

I looked at the gate, then at my legs. Trousers. Good. I had climbed plenty of gates and walls when I was a child. Not so many since, except when I was drunk, but the muscle memory should kick in soon enough. I climbed a couple of rungs, then swung my right leg over. The gate wobbled and swayed. I held still for a moment until it stopped moving, then swung my left leg behind me. In a series of quick movements, the heel of my left shoe caught on the gate, the gate wobbled, and I lost my balance and tumbled to the ground. Well, mainly to the ground. My right side hit earth, my left leg was still up in the air. The hem of my trousers was snagged on the top of the gate and I was in no position to unhook it.

Lumpy gravel was digging into my right shoulder, my right arm trapped under my side, my left arm waving wildly in the air and serving absolutely no purpose, and my glasses were somewhere in the long grass by the wall. The only noises I appeared capable of making were a series of curse words mixed with breathy, pathetic calls for help. No matter how hard I tried, I couldn't reach my left leg. I wiggled it in the hope that the fabric would rip and I would be released, but no, that wasn't working.

In the end, I gave up. I slumped down onto my back, one leg in the air, the other crumpled against the gate, and stared at the blurry sky above me.

A face appeared, a dark shape against the weak sun.

'*Argh!*' I shouted with surprise. The face laughed.

'You must really want to find me.'

'Danny?'

'The one and only. Hang on, I'll set you free.' He got my trouser hem uncaught and carefully lowered my leg to the ground. 'Are you hurt?'

'I don't think so. I also don't think I can get up.'

He offered me a hand and pulled me to my feet. 'Hang on.' He reached into the grass and handed me my glasses. I took them off him and put them back on.

'You could have just come when I called and I wouldn't have had to do that.'

'True, but it was quite funny.' Danny laughed again. I wasn't ready to laugh at myself.

'You and I need to talk.'

'Do we now, and why is that?'
'Because it's easier than talking to the police.'
He shrugged and started walking off.
'*Oi!* We need to talk.'
'Come on, then, I'll put the kettle on.'

23

'Tea?'

I screwed up my nose. 'Tastes like dishwater.'

Danny rooted around in a cupboard. 'Okay, then.' He sounded a little taken aback. 'Will this do? I've no idea when it last saw the light of day.' He held a cafetière in the air.

'Fine, thanks.' I felt something brush against my leg and quickly looked under the table. A Jack Russell was sniffing around my ankles.

'Oh, that's Daisy, don't mind her. She's quite friendly.'

'She probably smells my cat.'

'Don't tell me, you're one of those single women who treats her cat like it's her baby.' He was smiling as he said it and for some reason, I didn't leap out of my chair and stab him in the eye with a fork.

He looked back at the dog. 'I'd be careful, she's not a fan of cats.' I moved my foot away from her and he laughed. 'You'll be fine. Just don't meow or start purring.'

I really wanted to like this man, but I was also aware that I could very possibly be alone with a killer.

'You been hiding on the farm all along?'

'Yep, up in the barn for a lot of it.'
'Why did you show yourself to me?'
'Because Ben can't keep a secret to save his life...'
'Ben is?'

'My brother, and you were clearly keen to talk to me. The code to the gate is 1234, by the way. I'm surprised you didn't have a go before you tried climbing over. I'm glad you did that, though, it was much more entertaining. Also, there's no way you're the police.'

We sat in silence for a while as he made our drinks, eventually bringing a tray over and sitting across from me. He looked very like his brother. Better looking and a few years older, he had the same healthy look. His hair was tidier, but still long and wavy. Danny brushed it back behind his ears each time it fell across his face rather than peering at me from behind it.

'Why are you so keen to talk to me?'

'Because I found the body and I'd quite like to know why I found the body.'

'Ouch. Not very nice. You alright?'

'Fine, thanks, it's not my first.' He looked up mid-pour. 'It's not a big deal, it's just something that happens to me quite a lot.' He waited a beat, and then started pouring again.

'I'm not sure I want to know. I take that back, I definitely want to know, but I'm not sure I should.'

With our drinks ready, he looked me straight in the eye.

'I didn't kill Sheridan Tasker. I liked him, a breath of fresh air after that old-before-his-time fuddy-duddy.'

'Who do you mean?'

'Elliot Knight. Nice enough bloke, but he dresses like he's seventy.' I had to laugh at that.

'Okay, so you didn't kill Sheridan.' I intentionally tried to sound unconvinced. 'But the coins? You never wanted them to go to the museum in the first place, and you had access to them on your night shifts, and plenty of time to plan how you were going to get them out.'

'I didn't take them.'

'I don't believe you.' I swallowed. That had been rather brave of me, even Danny looked surprised.

He sighed and put his mug down. 'Why do you think I've been hiding? I know that I made a big deal about keeping the coins when I was young, thought they would make us a load of cash. I wasn't interested in history back then, I probably wanted the money to buy computer games. But I knew as soon as the coins went missing that I'd be blamed, and with Sheridan dead the same night, someone would be likely to connect the two and decide I was responsible for both.'

I had to admit, it was all very logical.

'Were you in the barn when I came to talk to your dad?'

'Yeah, he was in on it, agreed that I should stay out of sight until it all blew over.' He picked up Daisy and the dog settled down on his lap. A black patch of fur circled one of her eyes and she stared at me like a pirate deciding if I should walk the plank. Then she looked up and licked Danny's chin, destroying any tough image she was attempting to project. Danny kissed the top of her head.

'You one of those single blokes who treats his dog like it's his baby?' He laughed out loud, startling Daisy, who leapt off his knee. I couldn't help but smile.

'So, do you believe me?'

I thought for a moment, although mainly for effect. 'I do.' I could see his shoulders relax.

'So, what do I do now?'

'Talk to the police. They won't be impressed with you avoiding them, but I can see why you did it. Hopefully, they will too.'

'Hopefully?' He looked uncertain.

'I'm sure they'll tell you you've been stupid and haven't helped your case, it makes you look guilty, etcetera, etcetera, but I know a couple of them and privately, I'm sure they'll get it. Just don't tell them I said that.'

He looked distinctly nervous, but nodded.

'I know you're right. I'll give Dad a call, tell him what's happening, then I'll go to the police station.'

'I can give you a lift if you want.'

'Thanks, but I have a car.' He started to tap at his phone before stopping and looking at me. 'Actually, if you gave me a lift, would you come in with me?' He looked terrified now and I felt sorry for him.

'Of course.' I wasn't sure if Joe and Harnby were going to be pleased that I'd found Danny or angry at me for sticking my nose in. Either way, this was one avenue of investigation I was convinced they could shelve.

24

'I don't treat you like a baby, do I?'

Pumpkin was staring at me as I lay on the sofa, eating a digestive biscuit. I bit a tiny piece off, nibbled it around the edges so it was the right size and offered it to her. She sniffed it a few times, and then took it off my hand, chomping on it.

She looked up at me. 'Another?' I repeated the process, neatening the edges of the chunk of biscuit so it resembled the size and shape of her favourite cat treats. This time, she chewed and then sneezed, leaving my hand covered in biscuit crumbs.

'Pumpkin,' I moaned. I reached for a tissue and she stared at me. 'No more.' She glared. 'No.' She slunk out of the room.

After I'd left Danny at the station, I'd received a very stern telling-off from Joe, who informed me he wouldn't be letting Harnby know that I had delivered the missing man to the police. Whatever was causing her foul mood was still working its magic and apparently her head might explode if she knew I was involved. I promised I'd keep my head down, which was what I was doing as I lay on the sofa, eating biscuits and reading about museum thefts online.

I heard thunderous footsteps hammering down the stairs and nearly dropped my laptop as Pumpkin appeared close on the heels of a mouse, which dived behind the bookcase. Pumpkin went crazy, sniffing around the area and attempting to reach behind with her paw. Then she sat and stared. If it had any sense, the mouse would stay put and wait until Pumpkin got distracted by more easily accessible food. In the meantime, I had pulled my feet up off the floor, put the laptop down and stared with the same intensity as Pumpkin. I could try to catch it, but the chances were slim. My reactions were probably slower than Pumpkin's and she was a lumbering 18 pounds on a good day. I decided to maintain my current position on my little island and keep working. Pumpkin would let me know if the mouse stirred.

I managed to find a few references to thefts from the Pilston Museum, which included a collection of swords, some tapestries, and jewellery, but nothing that I could identify as useful or linked to recent events. The Duke had given me the impression that the number of thefts was much more extensive than that and I wanted to find out more. Mark would be able to tell me who we should talk to at the museum, or even within the Eyre family.

I was thinking about calling Mark when a small blur of brown skittered along the edge of the skirting board and behind the sofa. Pumpkin, whose eyes had been closed, only saw the movement at the last minute and shot to the sofa, where she came to a sudden stop. She couldn't fit behind it.

'There's motivation for you to lose weight.' I laughed, before realising the mouse could crawl up the back of the sofa at any time now, so I leapt across the room and made for the kitchen where I sat cross-legged on a chair to keep my feet off the floor. I jumped as my phone beeped and a message appeared on the screen.

'Pub?' It was Mark. *'Need to prepare for tomorrow.'*
'What's tomorrow?'

'The witch has landed.'
'What?'
'Joyce.'
'She didn't fly to Edinburgh.'
'Landed her broomstick.' I was going to save that message and use it to blackmail him should the need ever arise.

'OK, see you in pub in 15?' I didn't mind an excuse to get out of the house for a while, hopefully Pumpkin would carry out her feline duties while I was gone. That or the mouse would have let itself out the back door while Pumpkin slept.

'Umm, might take u longer.'
'What?'
'20 mins 4 you 2 get here 20 mins 4 us 2 get back.'
'What???? Where r u?'
'Museum.'

'Cheeky sod.' He was lucky that was all I said to him. He knew very well that I would drive out to fetch him. His excuse was that Bill was at a parents' evening. Mark could either call a taxi or get me, his own personal taxi service who would only charge him the price of a gin and tonic, to drive him around.

I stopped in a layby and messaged Mark when I was only a couple of minutes away from the museum. I didn't want to be hanging around waiting for him and he was notorious for faffing. I didn't get a reply and he still wasn't in the car park when I arrived, so I resigned myself to sitting and waiting. He had a remarkable ability to vanish into a piece of obscure history and for the rest of the world to melt away.

There was something rather haunting about the museum in the evening, especially one where the moon was shining a white glow through the trees. As soon as one moving shadow caught my eye, another would draw my attention. Dark shapes were cast across the red brick walls of the Victorian building. The steep-pitched roofs and high-peaked gables reached towards the sky. All it needed was the hoot of an owl and a deep American voice-over, and it would be the start of a rather corny horror film.

I very quickly got fed up with waiting. There was a faint glow of light coming from the far corner of the building and I knew that was the general direction of a side entrance, so got out of the car and walked towards it. I was on the side of the car park where staff were meant to park. The bushes were unkempt and the path that ran down the side of the building was a neglected alleyway, but any nerves were allayed by my knowledge that a couple of security guards were within shouting distance. Assuming, of course, that they weren't engrossed in a football match on the television. I cursed Mark as a tree branch took me by surprise and caught itself in my hair.

And then, I fell.

I was alright. I had grazed the palms of my hands and they stung, but that was the worst of it.

I looked back to see what I had fallen over, but the mound was hard to make out in the shadows. I thought I saw fur. Oh God, the museum's collection of taxidermied animals was creepy enough in a well-lit gallery. What was one of them doing out here? Or was it a dead fox?

The overhanging trees swayed a little in the night breeze, enough for me to realise that it wasn't actually fur I could see, but hair. Hair on a human head. I crawled round so I could take a proper look.

The mound was a person, face down, blood pooling beside their head. I moved closer, needing to see if they were still alive, and then I would run to the security office. I leaned in, trying to tell if they were breathing.

A stripe of cold white light moved across the body as the trees again swayed in the breeze. Yes, this person was breathing, but I wasn't. I was unable to take another breath as I recognised the body before me.

It was Mark.

25

'Where is he?'

I heard the words first, then I registered the clip-clop of heels clacking down the corridor, the sound hard, determined, the pace almost Olympian. I looked up from the cup of murky hospital coffee to see a vision of tartan striding towards me.

'I want to see him.'

'We need to wait, Joyce. The doctor's in there, checking him over.'

'He's conscious?'

'Yes.'

Joyce stared at the door and I took in the long tartan stole draped across her shoulders. The pattern matched that of the bag she clutched in her hand. Her shirt was a demure plain black, but her close-fitting ankle-length trousers continued the tartan theme.

'You just got back from hiding the Bonnie Prince?' My voice was flat and lacking in any energy. She ignored my attempt at humour and peered through the window in the door.

'I can't see him, the blasted doctor is stood in the way.' She swayed across the window, sampling every angle, huffing and puffing as she tried in vain to get a good view. 'When did you find him? Where was he? How bad are his injuries? Did you see who did it?' Not only was I not given time to answer each question, she didn't appear as though she would be listening anyway.

Eventually, she sat down next to me. 'I'll kill them.'

'I know you will, and I'll help.'

'I won't need help.' Joyce shot out of her seat and made for the door as the doctor came from the room. He stood blocking her way, as he hadn't even had a chance to get far enough out to close the door.

'I'm sorry, you can't go in yet. He needs his rest.'

'He would want to see me.'

'You'll need to return during visiting hours.'

Joyce stared at him. I could almost see the cogs turning as she decided which approach to take. She smiled and tilted her head a little.

'I've come all the way from Scotland...'

'I'm sorry, but it will need to be during visiting hours tomorrow.'

Joyce's charm clearly wasn't firing on full cylinders after the journey. Her face hardened. She was lining up another approach.

'Young man, I know for a fact that being surrounded by the support of friends and family can rapidly increase a patient's chances of recovery.'

'I'm sorry, madam, but...'

'It's alright...' Mark's voice came from behind the doctor '... you can let her in, she's my grandmother.'

I held my breath. If Mark wasn't already in the hospital, Joyce's response to that comment would likely have had him here in no time.

A sweet smile spread across her lips. 'Please, doctor. I won't tire him out.'

'Alright.' He looked at me. 'But just you, and not for long.' He stood aside and Joyce stepped in.

'My dear, sweet grandson...' was the last thing I heard as the door closed.

Minutes later, Joyce's head appeared out of the door like an expensively groomed ship's figurehead.

'Quick, get in.'

Mark looked pale, his forehead clammy, a line of stitches visible along his hairline, but he was still smiling, which I took as a good sign. Bill sat in a chair next to the bed, looking even more pale than Mark, and Joyce stood at the foot of the bed, watching over him like some kind of avenging angel.

'So, how was Scotland, bonnie lass?' Mark asked softly in a dreadful attempt at a Scottish accent. 'Get any of the local lads to show you their haggis?'

'If I had, I wouldn't tell you. Now, tell me who did this to you.' She was holding on to the rail at the end of the bed. Mark threw his hands up in the air.

'Your guess is as good as mine. The last thing I remember is leaving the museum by the side entrance. I said goodnight to Ian, the security guard, then walked towards the car park to wait for Sophie. I was a bit early, but it wasn't raining.'

That made me feel guilty for assuming he'd be late.

'Next thing I know, I'm waking up in the back of an ambulance. I did wonder briefly if we were on the way to the pub as planned, but no such luck.'

'Have the police been to interview you?' Joyce hadn't taken her eyes off him.

'Joe's been. Took some notes and said he'd be back in the morning.' I'd driven to Mark and Bill's to pick up a few things for the patient, after the ambulance had arrived on the scene, and I was very pleased to have missed Joe. After the right royal rollicking I'd received from him earlier, I was in no hurry for our paths to cross again.

'What did the doctor say?' Joyce asked Bill.

'Their initial assessment is that he was hit on the back of the head, probably with a big lump of wood, but it didn't do a huge amount of damage. The cut he got when he landed face first on the ground bled a lot, but only needed a handful of stitches. It was probably hitting his head on the floor that knocked him out. He's had a CT scan and a thorough going-over. He's bruised some ribs and might have concussion, so they want to keep an eye on him.' Bill sounded relatively calm, but he looked strained.

'How are you feeling?' Joyce asked the patient.

'I have a headache, and I'm rather perturbed that the doctors wouldn't use a nice feather stitch in turquoise thread, or perhaps a couple of lazy daisies. Make a feature of it.' He looked at each of us in turn. 'What? I would have ensured that my outfits matched the thread, I'm not a philistine... Oh, come on, it's not the first time someone's tried to kill me.'

26

I was pretty sure I felt my eyes popping out on stalks, and I thought that Joyce was going to have a seizure.

'What?' I gasped. How could he have neglected to tell me this? He had to be joking, surely? Another example of Mark's often dramatic sense of humour. 'When? You've never said anything about it. How many times has this happened? Actually no, my guess is you've lost count,' I said. 'Plenty's the time when I've wanted to run you over, push you off a bridge...'

'Hey, people, this is serious, we're talking about someone trying to kill me.'

'As opposed to the many who only thought about it,' I said. He crossed his arms and gave a dramatic display of sulking. Joyce threw me a stern look.

'She's finished now. If you feel up to it, Mark, we're keen to learn more.'

'An ex-girlfriend tried to run me over.'

'*Girlfriend?*' I wasn't sure which was the more shocking, that she'd tried to kill him or that she'd been, well, a she. I said nothing, but gave him an expectant look. Joyce looked thoroughly confused.

'I can't quite remember how we'd become a couple,' Mark continued. 'For the longest time, I thought we were just close friends, but it seems she thought different. When I eventually realised that she was expecting more from me, a lot more,' he pulled an expression of horror, 'I had to end things. I say end things, I wasn't aware I'd started anything, but when I tried to clarify, she was none too happy.'

'And tried to kill you?' I asked, needing to hear it again.

'She drove her car at me, twice. I can't think of any other objective, other than a bit of general maiming.'

At this point, I would have typically expected Joyce to come in with a jibe about how she'd have had better aim and there wouldn't have been a need for a second attempt. But instead, she shook her head and tutted.

'She must have been a very disturbed young woman. We can all just be extremely grateful that you have better taste these days.' She gave Bill a respectful nod. In return, Bill looked a bit bemused. None of us were accustomed to this version of Joyce.

'How did you get this to yourself?' I asked, suddenly noticing the luxury of a room outside of a general ward.

'I'm a celebrity, they're hardly going to put me in a ward with the masses, who I'd have to watch wander around with their bottoms poking out of their gowns. No, it's five-star service for me. That, or just old-fashioned luck, but right now I need all the positive thoughts I can get, so I'm working on the basis that they're all honoured to have me here and are treating me accordingly.'

Joyce had taken a seat on the opposite side of the bed to Bill.

'I'm glad to see you're in appropriate sleepwear. Who brought you your things? I do hope you have an eye mask; you must have an eye mask. Even if you can turn the light off in here, the glow from the corridor will disturb the quality of your sleep. What about skin care? The air in here will dry your skin.' She looked at the items on top of the cupboard by the bed. I'd grabbed toothbrush, toothpaste, the essential moustache wax and not much else. 'You need a delicate moisturiser and a night serum, I'll pick something up for you. Vitamins too.' She tapped away at her phone, making notes.

'We should probably go,' said Bill, starting to gather his things. 'We'll get kicked out before long anyway, and you should get some sleep, Mark. Is that alright?'

Mark smiled at his husband.

'Yes, you go. I'll be fine. Make sure these ladies get home safely.'

'I'll stay a little longer,' said Joyce. 'Bill, you go home, you need sleep too. You're going to be on Florence Nightingale duty for a while.'

'I don't need...'

Joyce ignored Mark's interruption and kept going. 'You too, Sophie.'

'Joyce, I'll be fine.'

She looked at Mark, her expression not one to be argued with. We said our goodnights, and Bill and I left them to it.

'She looks like Joyce,' he said as we walked towards the exit. 'Dresses like Joyce. Sounds like Joyce. But the words, do you think an alien has taken over her body?'

'It must be something in the Scottish air. Wait until tomorrow. Once she's had some sleep, the Joyce we know and love will be back.'

I sat in my car. I'd watched Bill drive off, but I'd been unable to do so much as turn the key in the ignition. I kept replaying the moment that I had realised the body on the ground was Mark.

Looking back, I was amazed I had been able to do anything but kneel by his side and stare, but somehow I had retrieved my phone from my pocket and called the police, and then shouted loud enough for Ian and his colleague to come out and see what all the fuss was about. It could have been so different. I could have been sitting in my car, trying to comprehend a future without Mark in my life. Instead, he was in the hospital with a couple of stitches and possible concussion. He was already smiling and making his characteristic cutting jokes, although he did look exhausted. He was going to be okay.

I repeated it to myself a couple more times.

He's going to be okay. He's going to be okay.

I knew that the person who had attacked Mark was the same person who had killed Sheridan. I was sure of it. I couldn't explain how I knew, but I was certain. I'd get a lecture off Joe, but I was determined to find who Mark's attacker, and therefore Sheridan's killer, was.

27

I'm not sure what time I woke up. About six, I think, which was obscenely early by my usual standards. Pumpkin was curled up so close that we had practically fused into one strange two-headed, six-legged animal. I reached out and rested my hand on her warm fur. But I didn't wake up with a start, remembering what had happened to Mark, mainly because I had been waking pretty much every thirty minutes throughout the night.

'I'm going to need a lot of coffee,' I groaned. Pumpkin moved slightly at the sound of my voice and I wiggled out the opposite side of the bed so as not to disturb her. I'd make the bed later when the queen had decided to get up.

Even just grinding coffee was hard work, but eventually I had a freshly brewed mug and buttered toast and I plonked myself at the kitchen table. As soon as I had sat down, Pumpkin jumped up onto the table and started rubbing her head against every part of my body she could reach. Eventually, she forced her way onto my lap and snuggled up against me, purring, her eyes watching my face.

'You're in a good mood this morning, and up early too.

Couldn't you sleep either?' She head-butted me. I drank my coffee awkwardly and off to one side in case she head-butted that, and I ended up in a room next to Mark with extensive burns.

My phone pinged with a message. It was Tina.

'I just heard about Mark, awful. Hope he's OK. We can cope fine at the house, don't come in. Keep me posted.'

I was so lucky to have someone like Tina working for me. I thanked her, telling her I would take her up on the offer. I didn't feel up to running a café today, let alone three, and in between visiting Mark, I had some work to do. Only it had nothing to do with serving cake to footsore tourists.

Pumpkin's head was still on the move, rubbing against my chin. This was not normal behaviour for this cat. She generally slept in until lunchtime, and then bossed me around for the rest of the day. Between Pumpkin and Joyce, there was something very strange going on. Maybe the aliens were taking over cats as well. I wondered if she knew, or had picked up on something in my demeanour. I was clearly out of sorts. I knew I'd woken her as I tossed and turned in the night, as she'd let out a little meow each time I moved.

Pumpkin eventually settled down, one paw resting on my arm, and glanced up at me from time to time. She was the perfect company while I gathered enough strength to go and take a shower. I hoped that something in her brain had been rewired and she would stay like this, but I wasn't going to bet any money on that.

I had to wait until 10am before I could go back to the hospital and see Mark, so the first thing I did was return to the museum. I needed to see the place where Mark had been attacked in the daylight. I don't know what I thought I would find, other than the area closed off by the police, which was exactly the scene I arrived to.

A young uniformed officer was making sure no one crossed the police tape. There was no sign of Joe or Harnby, and I was unspeakably relieved. The museum had yet to open to the public, so it was still quiet; just a few cars, which I presumed belonged to staff, were in the car park. I couldn't venture down the side of the museum, but from where I sat in my car, I tried to identify anything useful. This side of the car park was without cameras, and was where Elliot asked the staff to park. It was right next to a rough area thick with bushes and trees that overhung it. Mark's attacker could easily have thrown their weapon into the undergrowth, but that was likely to be the first place the police had looked.

A knock on my window startled me and it took me a moment to find the button to lower it.

'Sorry if I surprised you, I heard about your friend. I'm so sorry, I hope he's alright. Do you want to come and get a cup of tea?' Mimi had a kind face and I didn't have the heart to pull my usual expression of disgust at the offer of tea. 'I have something I want to show you.' With that final intriguing comment, she started to walk towards the horsebox-cum-café.

'Ian sent me a message about it this morning, just awful, really awful. Mark is so lucky it wasn't worse.'

Mimi set up a small metal table and matching pink folding chairs. They seemed insultingly cheerful for a day like today.

'I hope they catch who did it. He's a lovely man, always passes the time of day when he comes to get a drink or his lunch, and he's been so excited about the exhibition. I wonder if they'll delay it again and cancel the rescheduled reception.'

'I've no idea. I imagine if Mark feels up to it, he'll want it to carry on and he'll insist on being there for the party.'

'Yes, that sounds like him. A very determined young man, very energetic.' I made a note to tell him what Mimi had said. Hearing that someone had called him both young and energetic would probably have him back up on his feet in no time, and more insufferable than ever. I nodded, still thinking about the identity of Mark's attacker, although it was nice to be in Mimi's company. There was something rather calming about her, so different from the chaos that Joyce and Mark brought to my life. Wonderful, joyful chaos.

I felt a lump in my throat.

'You said you had something to show me?' I needed distraction, something practical to focus on.

'Yes.' She rooted around in the fabric tote bag she had kept with her. It looked like something she had made herself. 'When I arrived, I knew that I wouldn't be able to park where I normally do, near the alley at the side of the museum, and that parking would be limited.' She was still searching. 'I decided to park on the street, leave the spaces we have for the visitors. Well, I was walking across the car park and couldn't help but try and have a peek, so I got as close to the police tape as I could, and there at my feet I found something. Now, I know it wasn't there yesterday because that was where I parked and I would have seen it when I got in or out of the car. My usual spot wasn't free and I had to park right where some white paint had been spilt when the car park lines were repainted, so I know exactly where it was.'

She had finally found what she was looking for and put a scrunched-up handkerchief on the table. 'Hardly anyone carries a proper hanky these days,' she said, 'but my mother taught me to carry one at all times and I've continued to follow her advice.' From the way she smiled, I assumed that she had many happy memories of her mother.

Mimi slowly unfolded the pale blue handkerchief, displaying hand-embroidered flowers around the edge. As she peeled back the final corner, she revealed a key. A rather mucky key.

'I made sure I got none of my fingerprints on it, that's important, and I'm going to give it to the police, of course. But, well, I couldn't help but overhear one of your conversations with Mark and you seemed to be taking a lot of interest in Sheridan's murder.' She pushed the handkerchief and key in my direction and I peered down at it. 'I thought it was blood on it at first, but when I looked at it closer, well, I don't think it is. I think it's paint.'

She was right. It looked like paint all gathered up around the tip of the key, and it was the same colour as Elliot's car.

'It's been used to key a car,' I said, thinking aloud.

'Elliot's, by the look of things.'

'Yes, and if it wasn't there when you left yesterday, it was dropped last night, the same night that Mark was attacked. Maybe whoever killed Sheridan has it in for Elliot too, and was giving him some kind of warning, and the same person attacked Mark.'

'And the police will be able to identify the owner of the fingerprints on this key and they'll have the killer.' Mimi seemed a bit taken aback by that idea.

'I doubt they'll find any prints on it. The person who did this will have made sure of that. But it might give them something else to go on.'

I knew that Mimi had taken a chance by holding on to the key to show me before going to the police, but she had confirmed for me that I was on the right track.

28

I could hear Joe before I saw him. I took a deep breath and walked into Mark's room with a smile on my face.

Bill was sitting on one side of the bed, Joe the other, and Joyce in an armchair made of some kind of wipe-clean fabric in the corner, watching over everyone like Nurse Ratched minus the uniform. The police wouldn't need to worry about providing any protection, if Mark was deemed to need it; Joyce looked about ready to launch out of the seat and sink her claws into anyone who so much as sneezed in his direction. It was a little creepy.

I gave Mark a kiss on the cheek. I could smell the cedar wood fragrance of his moustache wax, which was pleasant and comforting. Then, I hugged Bill. When I turned to Joe, he was looking at me with the sort of expression that I had expected. Annoyed, very annoyed. He was typically a 'beer and slouch on the sofa' kind of guy, but today, he was straight-backed and had his legs crossed neatly.

'Sophie.' His voice was an octave or so lower than usual. This wasn't good.

'He's just been having words with us,' said Mark, adding air quotes around *having words*. Joe rolled his head back and stared at the ceiling.

'Is this still a joke to you?' His head snapped back down and he looked at his brother-in-law. 'Look at yourself, you're in the hospital and all because you two...' he swivelled his head between Mark and me '...can't stop sticking your noses in. This is serious, it's dangerous and now it's got one of you injured. You've had a couple of near misses in the past, but it was only a matter of time, and I keep telling you over and over again. Maybe I should have arrested you ages ago, it might have stopped you.'

'Unlikely,' said Joyce, sounding like she was on Joe's side.

'Don't you play the innocent either, you're just as bad.' Joyce looked shocked, but remained quiet.

Joe stood up and started pacing the room, which took about three steps for him to cross, so he looked a bit silly as he had to turn so frequently. I wished I'd sat down before he'd started his lecture. I felt like a naughty schoolgirl, didn't know where to look, where to put my hands. Could I put them in my pockets or would I look like I didn't care? Should I fold my arms or would that make me look defiant? My feet wanted to move, so I rocked them onto the sides of my shoes, then stood up properly again. No one seemed to notice. Joe continued and we all maintained a respectful silence.

'In fact, I've spent all morning trying to stop Harnby coming over here and arresting the lot of you.'

'What have I done?' said Bill, sounding confused.

'You spend a lot of time in their company, you're married to one of them, you've probably picked it up by osmosis.'

'Picked what up?' asked Mark, sounding just as confused.

'Stupidity. Blind, pig-headed, arrogant stupidity.'

'Hey!' Bill sounded annoyed at that comment.

'Maybe if Harnby were to arrest us all, we could get a family suite.' Mark looked up with a wide-eyed, hopeful expression.

'*Mark.*' Joe threw his hands in the air. '*You could have died!*'

'But I didn't.'

'I'm done, I'm just done.' Joe turned and marched out of the door. Mark, Bill, Joyce and I were frozen in place, silence washing over us.

'Do you think he's angry?' asked Mark eventually. 'I rather got that impression, but I can't be sure. Maybe I'm just particularly sensitive, it might be the drugs.'

'Joe's right.' Bill looked at me. 'This has gone too far, you need to let the police do their job.'

'You've known what we're doing all long, so you're an accomplice, just like Joe said,' commented Mark.

'Be that as it may, but you're in hospital.'

'Not for much longer.' Mark looked pleased.

'Why, are they letting you out?' I asked.

'They are indeed. Bill has a list of things to look out for in case I'm concussed. But other than that, I just need to take it easy for a week or so. The doctor will be round shortly to sign me off, and then I'm outta here. Have the engine running.' There was plenty of enthusiasm in his words, but it took effort for him to match them with genuine joie de vivre.

'I'm worried that it's too soon.' Joyce got up from the chair and opened the folder that was hooked to the end of Mark's bed.

'Do you understand any of that?' I wasn't aware she had any medical training, and the speed with which she flicked through the pages suggested it was unlikely she was actually reading anything.

'I understand enough.'

Bill caught my eye and gave his head almost imperceptible shake. I wondered what he and Mark had endured in her company before I arrived.

'So, Joyce, how was Scotland? Get up to anything interesting?' Bill's tone made it clear that we were moving on to a new subject.

'Very... interesting. We certainly weren't bored.'

'Find yourself a laird to sweep you off your feet and make you the lady of his estate?'

'I had a few offers.'

There was silence.

'Go on, then.' Mark pulled himself into a more upright position. 'Tell us more.'

'That can wait, you have a visitor.'

'Good morning.' The doctor scanned the room, taking us in one at a time. 'You're a popular man, Mr Boxer.' He glanced at the folder that Joyce had just returned to its holder. 'You are free to go home. I presume you will have someone with you for the next few days?' I saw Bill start to speak, but Joyce stepped forward and, before he had the chance to get his first word out, she informed the doctor that she would be monitoring Mark closely. Bill shot me a despairing look and I fought back laughter.

'Good. Take care, Mr Boxer.' And with that, the doctor was done.

Bill stood and pulled his shoulders back. 'Right, out, the pair of you. *I* will take *my* husband home. Joyce, you may visit later, for a short while. You wouldn't want to exhaust him and put his recovery back, now, would you?'

'I...'

'Would you?'

Joyce's lips became a narrow line. She grabbed her coat and a large tartan carpet bag and, after a final look at Mark, swept out of the room. I grinned at both men, and then followed her, having to run to keep up.

29

'You're not going.' Bill had walked into the sitting room just as we were discussing the official launch of Mark and Ananya's exhibition the following evening. 'You've only been home one night.'

'Yes, I am. I feel fine. You'll be with me, as will Sophie and my shadow over there.'

Joyce briefly looked up from her phone. 'Call me what you want, you can't say you've not been taken care of.'

'Because I wouldn't take care of him? Is that what you're saying?' Bill folded his arms and stared at Joyce.

'You're both doing a fabulous job and I wouldn't be feeling as well as I do without your love and support,' Mark said in a conciliatory tone.

'And me?' I chimed in. 'All the fresh pastries, gossip from Charleton House…'

'You have also…'

'I'm joking. I haven't the time to take on the job as your third servant.'

Mark had been home for twenty-four hours and was itching

to go out. He was already planning what he would wear to the evening reception.

'I have that new tweed waistcoat with the delicate thread of pale blue over-check. It's an exquisite fabric. I know which trousers will work with it and I'll wear my tan brogue boots. I have the perfect silk handkerchief for the pocket, oh, and the half hunter pocket watch I picked up the last time I went to London.'

Mark's eyes lit up as he spoke. He looked much less tired now, almost back to his old self. Bill sat down on sofa next to Mark and rested his hand on his thigh.

'I'm just worried and don't want you to set yourself back.'

'I feel fine.'

'The person who did this to you could be there.'

The silence that filled the room told me that everyone had thought the same. I know I had, but hadn't had the courage to say it out loud.

'Then there is even more reason for me to go. They failed, and I'm not going to be bullied into staying away from the museum. Besides which, there will be a lot of people around and they'd have to be pretty stupid to have another go in front of a crowd.'

'And I think they probably attacked Mark because he was quicker and easier to find than I was. They knew his whereabouts and could get to him much more easily.' Everyone turned to face me. 'I'm the one asking the most questions, I'm the one who always leads us into this kind of thing. I'm sure that given the opportunity, they would have bashed me on the back of the head and not bothered with Mark.'

'She's quite right,' said Joyce, with a certainty that made me wince.

'Then you should be careful too.'

I smiled at Bill. There had been real concern in his words.

'I know, and I will be. Like Mark says, there will be a lot of people at the reception. That's not to say that I think he should be going, but when he's already planned his outfit, I don't want to be the one who tries stopping him.'

Bill sighed, and Mark reached out and took his hand.

'I'll be fine, we'll all be fine. I've worked incredibly hard on this exhibition and I'm not daft – I know one of the reasons I got it was because of my profile, as small and local as that may be. I have an obligation to meet, plus the publicity will help me, and you know I want to do more of this kind of thing.'

'Alright, but you must promise to tell me if you don't feel well.'

Mark kissed his husband's hand. 'I promise.'

I drove back to Charleton House in time for the lunchtime rush, having left Joyce making the couple sandwiches. I hadn't been aware of her domesticated streak before and it had turned out she could make a pretty good Beef Wellington too, which she had presented for last night's dinner.

On the drive past dry-stone walls, overgrown verges and cows lazily chewing and not bothering to look up as I whizzed by, I realised how little thought I had given to Sheridan's death over the last couple of days. Despite the undeniable link between that and the attack on Mark, I'd almost forgotten about it. Maybe I was better off leaving it to the police. Apart from the risk I was putting my friends and myself in, I should be focusing on them, my job and my family. I wondered if it was time to back off. To let Joe and Harnby find out who had attacked Mark. Perhaps I was better off trying to make a soufflé without it sinking, and the last chocolate cake I had made had come out rather dry, so that required some practice. The Duke and Duchess would be hosting a Halloween ball next month and I was providing canapés and drinks. I should be turning my mind to horrors of the fake blood kind, to cakes with disturbingly real eyeballs or severed ears on top, bowls of punch that would make Dracula start to salivate. To mummies that... mummies that were actually real, recently murdered philanthropists?

I pictured Sheridan. Why would someone who had done so much good be killed? There I was again, going back to the murder. Chocolate brownies, blondies, flapjacks, little lemon tarts, custard slices, scones... I tried to reel off all the cakes I had seen in the case before I left the Library Café that morning in the hope that it would get me back on track. But it was no good. Sheridan kept popping back into my mind, the image of Mark lying motionless on the ground right behind it.

The police aren't having any luck either, I thought as I pulled up into a parking space next to the Charleton House stables. Or at least, I assumed not. I wasn't aware of any arrests, or even people being taken in for further questioning, and I wasn't going to ask, not after the mood Joe had been in the last time I saw him.

What is Joe's favourite cake? I thought. Maybe I could bake my way back into his good books.

30

It was nice to be at an event as a guest, not having to worry about providing any of the catering, or keeping an eye on the staff, and despite what I'd said to Mark about Mimi making the cakes, they were delicious. The opening reception for Mark and Ananya's exhibition was being held in one of the larger galleries at the Pilston, so we were surrounded by the museum's permanent collection of Egyptian artefacts that were always on display. The space where the new exhibition was housed was on the small side, so people milled in and out.

There were a number of recognisable faces as Mark had invited people from Charleton House, and the Duke was in attendance. The Duchess was still in London. Ellie Bryant from the conservation department – Joe Greene's girlfriend – was on the far side of the room, talking to Countess Eyre, the lady of Berwick Hall.

'Is Ryan here?' asked Joyce, her hand clasped around a champagne glass, each of her long fingernails painted with a different Egyptian symbol – the Ankh, the Eye of Ra, the Scarab beetle and more. 'It's time he and I had a proper conversation.'

'And what would that consist of?' asked Mark. 'Thumbscrews?

Demanding to know what his intentions are? The Spanish Inquisition lost a good woman when you retired.' He smiled at her with a kindness that didn't usually accompany his jibes. Perhaps he did have some lingering concussion. 'He sent me a card, you know, it arrived here this morning, wishing me luck and hoping that I was on the mend.'

Joyce nodded her approval.

'No, he's not coming. He's in Durham tonight, speaking at the university.' I was beginning to feel like someone with an imaginary boyfriend, made worse by the fact that his latest series was still running on TV so I really could be mistaken for someone making it all up to get attention.

Joyce eventually strutted off in the direction of the exhibition and Mark was cornered by a woman who was asking him so many questions, he'd yet to start answering any of them.

'You must be very proud of your friend.' The familiar voice of the Duke caused me to turn.

'I am, he's done an excellent job. They both have.'

'I do hope we don't lose him any time soon. But time does march on and I know he has aspirations for more than just guiding tours around our little home.'

'Little home with over 300 rooms,' I said, risking a spot of cheek with the Duke. Fortunately, he laughed in response.

We watched as a photographer took pictures of Mark and Ananya.

'How is he?' asked the Duke. 'It was such a dreadful thing to happen, I'm not sure I'd want to return to the scene in a hurry.'

'I'm not sure he would have done had it not been for this event. I think he's alright, but you know Mark. He's very good at putting on an act.'

'Agreed. However, he does seem to have his own personal bodyguard now, so I doubt any further harm will come to him.'

I looked in the direction of the Duke's nod, expecting to see Joe hovering near Mark. Instead, I saw Joyce watching him like the proverbial hawk, occasionally scanning the room around him.

'I actually think that Joyce might also have had a bump on the head.'

That made the Duke laugh again. 'That woman is quite something, and I mean it in an entirely positive way. Not many people get to see to the core of her, of that I'm certain, but I think we're getting a glimpse of it now.' He raised his glass a little, and then backed away, melting into the crowd of guests.

I watched as Ian snaked through the room. No doubt security was extra alert tonight. He stopped and whispered into a woman's ear, and she smiled.

'Who's that?' I asked Mark, who had returned to my side. 'The woman talking to Harriet Tasker. Ian seems to know her.'

'That's Libby, she was Sheridan's secretary.' The woman looked to be in her sixties, grey hair in a smart but rather unadventurous style. A dark pastel-pink dress hung loosely, reaching her shins, a simple leather bag dangling from her shoulder. 'I imagine she's been here on a number of occasions with Sheridan and knows the staff. Now, have you seen Bill? He said he was going to get me another drink – my last of the evening, apparently.' His final few words were spoken in a deep sulk. 'Unless you…'

'Not a chance. I'm amazed Joyce is letting you have any at all.'

Mark took a quick glance over his shoulder. 'She's not. We're having to be rather surreptitious about it.' I gave him a wide-eyed *be careful* stare.

'Well done, Mark, it's a superb exhibition.' Lord Eyre had appeared, taking me by surprise. 'You've really captured my grandfather's adventurous spirit, and you've kept it in the style of the museum. I know that Ananya has really enjoyed working with you.'

'And I with her,' replied Mark. 'She has a real love for Berwick Hall.'

'Indeed she does. Her tours always receive superb reviews. How are you, anyway? So sorry to hear about your incident.'

'I'm fine, no real harm done.'

'Well, I hope they catch whoever did it.'

I decided to take this opportunity to quiz the lord. 'When the police do catch whoever attacked Mark, we can safely assume that they have also caught Sheridan's killer.'

Lord Eyre wore a thoughtful expression as he nodded. 'I can see why you would think that, yes, it does make sense.'

'Was Sheridan's death a complete surprise to you, or did you ever hear about him getting involved in things that you might consider risky?'

He looked taken aback. 'Are you asking me if Shed was a crook?'

'No, no, I just mean he might have inadvertently got involved with something dangerous, or perhaps he was being blackmailed.' I was relying on Mark's description of Lord Eyre as a nice, down-to-earth chap and hoping he wouldn't fly off the handle at me. He didn't look happy at my questions, but did at least appear to be giving them some thought.

'You're not the first to ask me that. But no, I can't think of anything. Now, if you'll excuse me, there are a few people I must say hello to.'

'You took a bit of a chance there,' said Mark as we watched his retreating back.

'True, and he seemed keen to avoid any further conversation. Do you think that might be significant?'

'I don't know. But he and Sheridan had known each other from the museum for years, and they mixed in many similar circles. Sheridan was new money, but he was generous with it and they'd have attended many of the same fundraising events.'

'Ladies and gentlemen... Ladies and gentlemen...' Elliot struggled to make himself heard above the hubbub of the crowd.

He clinked a couple of glasses together, and eventually someone with a much louder voice broke through.

'Ladies and gentlemen, Elliot Knight, Director of the Pilston Museum.' A round of applause followed and everyone turned to look at Elliot, who was standing at the top of some steps that led to a wooden door marked 'Private'.

'Sheridan once said to me that although he loved the objects in the Pilston, and he loved the building, it was the people who mattered the most to him. The people whose stories are told through the objects, the people who put brick on top of brick to create this fine building, the people who work here and, most importantly, the people, young and old, who visit and share this magical collection with us. I know that Sheridan would have been in awe of this superb exhibition and the skilled way in which it tells the stories of important people and objects. I wish to thank and congratulate Mark Boxer of Charleton House and Ananya Shah of Berwick Hall...'

As Elliot continued his speech, I looked around the room. Mark, listening intently and giving Ananya a quick glance and a wink. Bill, watching Mark with a look of pride, matched by Joyce's expression of fondness, which softened her face in a way I couldn't recall seeing before. The Duke and Lord Eyre nodding from time to time in response to something Elliot had said. Harriet Tasker, looking sadly into her glass of wine, but glancing up and smiling with each reference to her husband.

Then there was Libby, Sheridan's assistant. She was standing at the back of the crowded room and I watched as she glanced around a few times, and then slunk out.

31

'I want to know what you're doing about Mark.'

I looked up from cleaning the counter in the Stables Café. It was quiet and I had decided to spend some time with the staff there as, if I was honest, I did tend to neglect them a little. That, and I was tired after last night's reception and was avoiding the long queues in the Library Café.

A well-manicured fingernail tapped on the wooden surface. 'What do you have so far?'

I'd known her for a little under four years, but Joyce still had the ability to terrify me. When you're confronted by a woman who looks as if she is about to face the English forces at Culloden and rewrite history in the process, you can be forgiven for taking a gulp and checking where the closest exit is. Her dress looked like two had been stitched together down the middle, one half dominated by an orange- and lime-themed tartan, the other plain black. A belt pulled her middle in so tight, I was surprised she could breathe. The points on her orange stilettos could be classified as weapons, along with her nails.

'What am I doing about Mark? He's not under suspicion, is he?'

'You know very well what I mean. I want to get my hands on whoever it was that attacked him and you must have some ideas.'

I sighed, mouthed *sorry* at the staff member who was enjoying a well-earned break, removed my apron and walked with Joyce out into the courtyard of the stables. It was quiet, having only just stopped raining. She turned to face me and her shoulders fell a little. With a quieter, softer voice, she repeated her question.

'Do you really have no idea who might have done this?'

I shook my head. 'We keep hitting dead ends. I'm certain it must be the same person who attacked Sheridan, and now they seem to be warning Elliot off, but I'm not getting anywhere. Maybe we should leave it to the police.'

'And are they close to catching who did it?'

'I don't know. I've not seen much of Joe, other than when he read us the riot act, and if what he says is anything to go by, we might be best off avoiding Harnby. Something or someone has got her in a foul mood. There is one thing, though.'

Joyce's head snapped round to face me. 'Out with it, girl.'

'Libby, Sheridan's assistant. She snuck out of the reception last night, during Elliot's speech, and bearing in mind a lot of what he was saying was about her boss, you'd think she would have hung around.'

'Then what are you doing here?'

I knew there was only one way to answer that.

'I'm on my way. Are you coming?'

'Of course not. Mark has insisted on coming into work for a couple of hours, so I'm working from his office. Someone needs to keep an eye on him, make sure he doesn't have some sort of delayed concussion.'

I watched her stride confidently across the cobbles, a surface that would give most stiletto wearers a twisted ankle. It seemed I had no choice but to abandon my staff, again.

. . .

I pulled into the car park of the Tasker biscuit factory, a vast red-brick building. Built during the First World War, it had architectural style, something that couldn't be said of modern factories. Located on the outskirts of Macclesfield, it was a major employer for the area.

Despite selling the business, Sheridan had maintained an office for his philanthropic foundation, and although he hadn't spent a great deal of time there, it was where Libby had a desk. As I turned off the ignition, my phone buzzed with a message from Mark.

'Libby is married to Ian Wiggins, museum security.' So, that was why he was whispering in her ear in such a friendly way. It still didn't explain why she had slipped away during a speech which was partly honouring her boss, though. She hadn't looked like the most friendly of people, but I really hoped that particular appearance would be deceptive and she would talk openly with me.

The sweet aroma of baking biscuits filled the air. I wondered if those who came here regularly were able to identify what was on the production line that day by the smell alone. I thought I might get a bit sick of it after a while. The entrance for visitors was easy to find and I was buzzed straight through and given instructions on how to find Libby. She was waiting for me at the door when I arrived. A look of recognition crossed her face.

'Please come in. I know you, don't I?'

'I was at the Pilston Museum last night.'

She didn't say anything in response, indicating a chair for me and offering me a drink, which I declined. The office was impeccably tidy and rather dull. It felt like a relic from the 1970s. A grey filing cabinet stood in one corner, brown carpet tiles covered the floor. I couldn't imagine Sheridan spending a lot of time here. He was much more stylish, or had seemed that way. Perhaps he left Libby to keep the office however she wanted.

'I can't imagine why you want to see me.'

'If I'm honest, I'm not entirely sure myself. I do know I want to find out why Sheridan was killed.'

'Isn't that the job of the police?'

'Yes.' I chose not to elaborate. There was something watchful about Libby. I had the feeling that if I said too much, I might find it used against me. Cautious but direct, seemed to be the way to go. 'Do you have any idea why someone would want to kill him?'

'No. As I told the police, I can't think of anything, although I was not party to all aspects of his life.'

'Did he talk much about his work at the museum?'

'Yes, in the same way that he talked about all of his projects to me. I'm… I was his administrative assistant, so I was aware of almost everything he was working on. He often asked my opinion and I regularly took minutes in his meetings.'

'Then you must have been able to offer him some very valuable insight, being married to someone who works at the museum.'

'Ian's work doesn't impact on the project that Shed was involved with. Shed did ask me to run a few things by him, to get an idea for how staff might feel about some aspects of the project, but that was as far as it went. A security consultant was brought in to advise on that side of the new building.'

I didn't know what it was about this woman that made me so uncomfortable, but it was probably the same personality trait that would have made her invaluable to Sheridan. I imagined that she was a superb gatekeeper, keeping all unwanted attention at bay. The Duke and Duchess had someone like that at Charleton House. Terrifying and efficient.

'Does Ian ever mention someone by the name of Kit Porter to you? He's a member of the museum staff who opposed the renovation, and I believe he can be rather outspoken about other issues too.'

I could see that Libby was trying to fight back a smile. The corner of her mouth was twitching and she glanced away briefly before answering.

'Oh yes, he's talked about Kit. The man really doesn't do himself any favours. I have no doubt that he has the best of intentions at heart, but sadly, he only makes himself a lot of enemies. Even those who agree with him don't wish to be associated with him, and those who do spend time with him are...' She paused and seemed to give this a lot of thought. 'Let's say they are followers, not the most strong-willed of people.'

'How far did his opposition to Sheridan's project go?'

'Do you mean might he have killed Shed to stop it going ahead? I really don't know, but there is a very definite mean streak in the man. I've only met him a couple of times, but that was the impression I came away with. I believe there was some talk that he might have been behind a voodoo doll of Elliot.'

Libby was the second person to suggest that Kit might be responsible for the doll – make that three if Ian was of the same opinion. I needed to look more closely at Kit. Had his mean streak really extended to murder? Or had one of his followers taken their loyalty too far?

'Now, if you'll excuse me, as I'm sure you can imagine there has been a great deal of correspondence for me to respond to following Shed's passing and I really must carry on with my work.'

Libby stood, making it clear the meeting was over.

'Just one more thing,' I said as I gathered my belongings, trying to make it appear like a casual question. 'You left the reception during Elliot's speech last night – a speech that was to a large extent talking about Sheridan.' That brought the woman up sharply and I could tell she hadn't realised she had been spotted sneaking out. 'Didn't you want to stay and listen to it all?'

'Of course I did. Something came up.'

She practically pushed me out of the door and shut it firmly behind me. I had rattled her.

32

*M*ark was at his desk. He looked as well put together as ever, if a little more casual; a pair of jeans had been paired with a pale blue shirt and tweed waistcoat. His healthy glow was back and his moustache perfectly curled at the ends. Opposite him at an abutting desk, Joyce had set up a laptop.

'Thank God, reinforcements are here,' he said desperately as I walked in with three takeout coffees and a bag of chocolate croissants. 'Lady Macbeth here is taking the role of jailor, sorry nurse, far too seriously. I daren't sniff for fear she'll lean over the desk with a tissue like the mother of a toddler, I daren't go to the bathroom while she's here in case she follows me and…'

'I don't need to hear any more, but thanks all the same for putting the image in my head. I'm beginning to regret coming now.' I handed the refreshments around. 'Does Bill know you're here?'

'God, no. He's out at a match with his kids' rugby team and I promised him I'd work from home, but I was going stir-crazy. I've sworn Joyce to secrecy, but I'm worried she's going to use it against me.'

Joyce eyed him over the top of her reading glasses. I settled myself into a vacant office chair and told them about my visit to the Tasker factory.

'Libby's hiding something, but I don't know what.'

'Might she be having an affair?' Mark raised a good question, but I saw one key problem with that.

'Ian was at work last night. It's a huge risk to sneak off and see Romeo when your husband is in the building, let alone the nerve it would take to have an affair with someone at your husband's workplace at all.'

'Very risky.' Joyce nodded knowingly.

'Something you want to tell us?' asked Mark.

'*Moi*? Innocent as the driven snow. The question is, do you think what she is hiding is murder?'

'I don't know. I have no doubt that if you crossed her, she could make you suffer,' I replied.

'Who does that leave us with?' Mark was turning slowly from side to side on his chair. I started to count on my fingers.

'Libby, one. Danny Jones, two. There was a time when he didn't want the coins to be given to the museum, so if he was trying to steal them back, Sheridan might have seen him and been collateral damage.'

'But you don't believe it was him,' Mark acknowledged.

'Agreed, I'd strike him off the list entirely. I don't think he stole the coins either. There is Kit Porter, three, who may or may not have made a voodoo doll in Elliot's image, and might have a vendetta against the management of the museum.'

'Working on the basis that Kit did make the voodoo doll, then that could also make him the person who keyed Elliot's car. The two things could be put in the same category of vindictive behaviour.' Joyce had mimed scraping a key along the side of a car as she talked. She looked as if she was familiar with the action.

'But that would mean there is a strong chance that it was him who attacked me,' said Mark. 'After all, Mimi found the paint-covered key not far from where I was hit, but I don't know why Kit would want me dead.'

'Because you and I are asking questions about the murder of Sheridan. Whoever the killer is could want you dead for that.'

'Do you think Libby was having an affair with Sheridan?' Joyce asked.

'I didn't even think of that. She's utterly unlike his wife, so I don't know what he'd see in her.'

Mark shook his head. 'That feels like grasping at straws. But what if we look at it from a different angle? Sheridan was having an affair with someone we feel is more likely, his wife found out and she killed him?'

'When I met her, she seemed genuinely distressed, so I find that hard to imagine. Plus security said there was no one in the museum who didn't work there during the time that Sheridan was killed.'

'Ha!' Mark exclaimed. 'You're assuming that any guest would have signed in or shown their face to security. They're not the most conscientious guards – they were watching football, for heaven's sake. Godzilla could have charged in through the front doors and they wouldn't have noticed. I never signed in once, even before it was confirmed that I would work on the exhibition and I got a temporary staff pass.'

Mark rubbed his forehead.

'Are you alright?' Joyce demanded and started to stand. Mark looked confused.

'What? I'm just thinking. I'm fine, sit back down, woman.' He looked at me. 'See?'

'You love it.' I laughed and noted that he didn't argue with me. 'Look, we're getting nowhere fast. Mark, can you try and find out more about Sheridan? Maybe he did something in the past that was controversial and had links to the museum.'

I made my way to the door.

'What should I do?' asked Joyce. It was at that moment Mark decided to have a final spin in his chair and went a little too fast, almost falling on the floor. Joyce tutted. 'You don't need a short-term nurse, you need a full-time carer.' Mark grinned and I left him dabbing coffee off his shirt.

33

Mark's office overlooked one of Charleton House's courtyards, a dreamy, picturesque view, especially when it was closed to visitors and you could imagine the ghosts of past residents crossing the cobbles. I felt like I'd seen a spectre myself when I descended the stairs and stepped out into the cool post-rain air. Heading my way was Detective Constable Joe Greene.

'You might want to check on him another time, he has his personal bodyguard in there and if you put a foot out of place, she'll eat you whole.' I was hoping that if I kept things light, I wouldn't get the telling-off that I knew was coming, and which I deserved. Joe stopped in his tracks and stared in the direction of the stairs to Mark's office. He grimaced.

'Reckon I'll come with you, I wanted a word. I'll go and see Mark tonight.'

We walked in awkward silence, Joe eventually being the one to break it.

'How's it going with Ryan?'

'I'm not sure it's going at all. He's on his book tour. We've spoken a couple of times, but I don't know when I'll next see him.'

'Mark likes him, so he's passed that test.'

'Mark is in awe of him, he wants to be him, so he's hardly the best judge.'

'True, but at least you won't have to worry about your friends getting on with him. Not that friend anyway.' We'd arrived at the Library Café and Joe took a seat in a corner. I sat opposite him. I had to face whatever was coming my way.

'Sophie, what I said at the hospital…' I readied myself for some strong words. 'I meant every word, but I'm not going to repeat myself. However, Mark is family, and that's how I consider you, and Joyce in some weird, twisted way, and I worry about you all. I want you to stop taking risks. I also know you'll ignore me, but I have to say it, so there we are, I have.' The look in his eyes sent a stronger message than any words could. 'Also, I know you went to see Sheridan's assistant at the Tasker biscuit factory, so you're already ignoring me.'

'How much harm am I going to come to at a biscuit factory? I suppose I could get pushed into a huge vat of dough, but it's unlikely. How do you know about that anyway?'

'A retired PC I used to work with does part-time work on their security team and he gave me a call. Let's just say you've come up in conversation over a pint on occasion and when he heard you say you were from Charleton House, he knew exactly who you were, thought he'd give me the heads-up.'

'Well, if it makes you feel any better, I don't have a clue who killed Sheridan, or who attacked Mark.'

'And you're giving up?' He gave me an exaggerated look of hope.

'I'll say yes because that will also make you feel better.' I decided it was time to change the topic. 'Have you found out what's going on with Harnby yet, why she's in such a bad mood?'

'Yes, I have. It turns out that DI Flynn is retiring, which opens up a chance for Harnby to climb up the next rung on the ladder. I guess that she's either stressing out trying to decide whether or not to go for it, or going for it and worrying that she might not get it. I'm not sure what the fuss is about. She should go for it, she's perfectly qualified. She just needs to get on with it.'

I let my head loll to one side and stared at him.

'Joe, I would put money on the fact that as a female officer, let alone a gay one, she has to work harder than any male officer, make sure she's proven herself more than a male officer would, that she does all she can to avoid making mistakes because she can't risk a single one. She's probably afraid of getting the job, and then screwing up, or people thinking she's not capable. Besides which, women are more inclined to think they're not qualified for a job, even when they are. You blokes see a job that's wildly out of your reach and think *yeah, I reckon I can do that, bring it on.*'

I ended the sentence doing my best blokey impression. Joe was staring at me, mouth slightly open.

'So give her a break, and maybe it's not that. Maybe something else is going on. Either way, be nice.' I knew that the Detective Inspector in question was Harnby's uncle, something she'd managed to keep from Joe and the rest of the team at the station. So, I guessed that she was also worried that if she got the job and people found out about the link, they would assume that some kind of nepotism was at play. It was probably added pressure. 'I assume you'll go for sergeant if she moves up?'

'Yeah, 'course, I passed my exam, I'm ready.' I grinned, at which I could almost hear the cogs of his brain turning. 'Ah, rather proven your point, haven't I?' I nodded.

'It would be great to have you stay in the area, though, and I'm sure Ellie would be pleased.' A smile travelled across his face. 'Things are going well there?'

'Great. Actually – and don't say anything, I've not told anyone else yet – I'm thinking of asking her to marry me.'

That floored me.

'Wow, congratulations, or good luck, whichever. That's exciting.' It was exciting, but there were so many emotions hitting me from all sides that I couldn't work out what I felt.

'I know, terrifying too, and I need to get a ring. But yeah.'

'You should ask Joyce.'

'To marry me?'

'No, to help you choose a ring.'

'Are you trying to sabotage my chances of Ellie saying yes? I don't want to strap a Fabergé egg to her finger.'

'You should give Joyce a chance. I know her taste is a little on the gaudy side, but she does know her stuff and is actually quite respectful about what someone might like.' Joe stared at me. 'Well, most of the time. I'm serious.'

'I know you are and that's what worries me. Are you sure you weren't the one hit on the head, not Mark?'

'Ah, you're joking about it, you must have forgiven me.'

'I'm not and I haven't, but it's the only explanation I can think of.'

'Talk to her, I think she'll be able to help.'

A look of deep concentration was etched on his face.

'Alright, I will. It can't be scarier than dealing with Harnby right now.'

34

Mimi was writing up a list of cakes on a blackboard and drawing ornate flowers in the corners, but she looked up as I crunched across the gravel towards her. She smiled.

'I'm making the most of a lull to freshen things up a bit.' She started to stand.

'No, no, stay where you are, it's okay. I wanted to talk to you.'

'Then pull up a chair, you've picked a good time. Mind if I carry on? Now I've started, I better get it finished.' I watched her for a moment as she delicately picked out the lines of dahlias in the top corners, lavender in the bottom ones. There was no doubt that she was a talented artist.

'So, what is it I can help you with?'

'Kit Porter. I'd like to know more about him.'

'You want to know if he really is capable of killing someone, or if that's just gossip from a bunch of people who don't like him and have had to put up with his complaints and rabble-rousing for far too long?'

'That pretty much sums it up, yes.'

Mimi put her chalks down and turned to face me.

'I'm convinced that it was Kit who sent the doll. Yes, I have no doubt about that, and that makes him a man with an evil streak. Voodoo dolls are cruel and to some extremely frightening. Also, think about it – we work in a museum where there has been talk of a curse. We know how seriously some people take that sort of thing. And apart from the effect on the person who is the subject of the doll, imagine how it makes everyone else feel. It's not a nice place to work if that sort of thing happens, is it. If Kit's capable of sending the doll, then he's capable of damaging Elliot's car, and he's more than capable of ransacking Elliot's office.'

That was news to me.

'When did that happen?'

'Last night, or this morning. When Elliot arrived for work, he found his office in a terrible state.'

'So, he really is the target, then. Surely that means the killer had intended to attack him, that Mark wasn't the true target the other night and they made another unsuccessful attempt to kill Elliot. But could Kit get in and out without being seen? Everyone would recognise him on cameras or if they ran into him.'

'And surely that's the point. He would blend in. He makes a nuisance of himself everywhere in the building, so no one is surprised to see him in the strangest of places and his presence wouldn't appear unusual. He often starts early and finishes late, doing paperwork related to the various complaints he's making against the museum. He's been here years, he knows every short-cut, where every camera is. He knows the routines of the security teams. He's even helped out in the security office when they've been short-staffed, and he lives just round the corner so he could go home and sneak back quickly. But I have to admit that the idea of him stealing items is more than I would have thought him capable of. He's obsessed with this place, so I don't think he'd do anything to damage the collections.'

'Hang on, what are you talking about?'

'The items that were stolen last night. As well as Elliot's office being ransacked, the intruder got away with a couple of very rare watches that had been removed from display for cleaning.'

This was a lot to take on board. I needed to talk to Kit myself.

'Hi, Sophie, is Mark here?' Ananya was heading my way across the car park.

'No, he's at Charleton House, I had business of my own here.'

'Did you hear about the break-in last night? It's so sad, after such a wonderful evening, and then we wake up to more bad news. I'm starting to think there might be something in that curse.' She looked away as she spoke and waved before turning back to me. I couldn't help but look to see who she had waved at. Kit was walking towards the road.

'You know Kit?'

'From the museum, yes.'

I decided there was no harm in finding out if any useful information had made its way to Ananya.

'Do you know much about him? What kind of a man is he?'

She looked about to answer, and then paused, glanced down at her feet and back at me.

'I don't know him well, I just see him around here and he's very knowledgeable and good with the visitors.' She glanced in the direction of the road, where Kit had just walked out of sight.

'What is it? Do you know something about him?' She looked a bit guilty and I wondered if maybe they were dating, or had done in the past. Not that I would ever have put them together, so I'd be amazed.

'He interviewed for a job at Berwick Hall a few years ago.' I waited for her to continue. 'He didn't get it, there were a couple of candidates who were more qualified than him. It involved managing people and he had no experience of that.'

'Really? I mean, I'm surprised he applied for a job anywhere else. From what I've heard, he'll have to be carried out of the

Pilston in a box. Sorry, that was very inappropriate, but from everything I know about him, he's a diehard Pilston man.'

'It was a short-term project, a bit like the work Mark and I have been doing here, and Kit made it *very* clear that his loyalties were to Pilston and he wouldn't be looking to make a permanent move. The work also involved a crossover between the Pilston and Berwick Hall, so on paper, he was ideal.'

'Was his lack of management experience the only problem?'

'I really shouldn't be telling you this, it's confidential.'

I tried to make eye contact with her. 'What is it, Ananya? Does it relate to what's been happening here?'

'No! Heavens, no, at least I don't see why it would.'

I wanted to scream and just drag it out of her.

'He didn't get the job because, like I said, he didn't have the relevant experience, but he also had a criminal record. It didn't impact on our decision – we would have been happy to give him a chance if he'd had more experience, but now whenever I see him, I just find it a bit weird. I don't know if he realises I'm aware of his past.'

My stomach flipped, but not in a fun, excited way. It was in an 'oh heck, I need to sit down' kind of way.

'What did he do?'

'A misspent youth stealing cars.'

'Oh, so he hasn't killed anyone,' I joked, and then immediately felt bad. Ananya didn't answer. 'What?'

'Not exactly.'

'Come on, Ananya, what does that mean?'

'A car that he and some friends had stolen hit and killed a pedestrian. He wasn't driving, though.'

'Presumably the Pilston would know that from when he applied. He would have had to declare a criminal record to them too.'

'He might not have declared it, if he felt it was stopping him from getting jobs, and then it depends on how thorough Pilston was about getting references and doing checks. I'll be honest, I don't get the impression that things are that organised here. The other thing is that when he applied for the job at Berwick Hall, he used his full name Christopher, which I guess would be on his police file. There was nothing to indicate that he went by Kit when he came to us. Look, I need to go, but will you keep that to yourself?'

'I can't promise that, Ananya, what if it's relevant to this case?'

She looked wide-eyed with surprise.

'How could it be connected? He was stealing cars, not breaking into museums, and it was a long time ago. And the death was an accident, he wasn't behind the wheel. Shouldn't we all be given a second chance?'

'Yes, we should.'

'I need to go, sorry to rush off.'

I watched her head to the main entrance and wondered if she was right and there was no link. I also wondered if Joe knew about Kit's misspent youth.

35

I was starting to feel a slight nip in the air in the evenings. Autumn was definitely knocking on the door, and in response I had lit a fire for the first time since spring. It took me a while to get it going. I was out of practice, and I spent so much time on the floor as I tried that my knees didn't want to unlock when I attempted to stand. Eventually, I managed it, to the accompaniment of a click that I was hearing more and more when I got up from a kneeling position. Old age was heading my way, closely followed by the black-cloaked figure of death.

Wow! That was morbid, even for me. Maybe it was a sign that I was spending too much time thinking about murder.

I made myself comfortable in the armchair and heard an elephant thudding towards me. By elephant, I mean Pumpkin, whose footsteps are so loud that I have, on occasion, been convinced that there is another human in the house – a human who has not been invited. She sat in front of the slowly growing flames.

'Thanks, Pumpkin, you're going to block the heat.' She didn't even turn to acknowledge my rude comment. 'Has your tiny little pal left you? Gone home? Concluded that I have no cheese and it's not worth sticking around? I'm going to work on the basis that it wasn't all that afraid of you, you are somewhat hindered by your size.'

I took her silence as agreement, or annoyance at my final comment.

'How is it,' I asked her, 'that everything happens at once? Mark ends up the victim of a horrific attack, Joyce turns into a scary Florence Nightingale, both Joe and Harnby could end up with promotions, Joe is planning on proposing to Ellie. The world has been turned upside down.'

Pumpkin settled down into the familiar loaf position, paws tucked into her body, nose as close to the heat as she dared.

'You are the one thing I can rely on not to change, get wrapped up in drama or be on the receiving end of someone else's drama. Okay, so you've spent the last few days turning this house upside down in the hunt for a mouse and I'm at constant risk of stepping on its remains, but I suppose by your standards that's normal cat business, which proves my point even further. You appear to be my rock, my port in a storm, my little fur-covered bundle of sanity. Okay, not little, but you get my point.'

She didn't stir and I was becoming increasingly aware of the fact that I was talking to a cat whose general disdain for me meant that she would probably trip me up at the top of the stairs long before she willingly took on the role of my comforter. I was also aware that she wasn't up for a chat, whether that meant small talk or in-depth discussions on the meaning of life, so I phoned Mark.

'Pumpkin isn't interested in speaking to me and I need to discuss something with someone, mull it over, talk something through out loud, query a quandary.'

'Have you been drinking?'

'No.' He couldn't see the rather large gin and tonic in my

hand, and there was no one here to tell him about it, unless Pumpkin suddenly got chatty.

'Hmm. Well, what is it you want to mull over, free from the influence of alcohol?'

'Joe.'

'You've changed your mind, you do want to marry into the family.'

That stunned me into momentary silence.

'No, why would you think that? And anyway, he seems to have plans in that department. No, I wanted to ask him if he's aware of something in relation to the case, but there is a strong chance that he already knows so I'll look foolish, or he doesn't know and I might make him look incompetent, and either way he'll get annoyed that I'm sticking my nose in after he gave us such a strong warning.'

'What is it?'

'It turns out that...' I thought about Ananya's request that I didn't tell anyone, and she had to work with Mark who probably wouldn't be able to remain quiet. 'I can't say.'

'Really? It's me, come on.'

'No. Maybe later, when I know whether it's important or not.'

'Huh, I'm offended. Alright, if it could be important and he doesn't know, then you have to tell him.'

'Could you tell him?'

'I have to sit at the table with him at family dinners. No. And anyway, how can I tell him if I don't know what it is?'

'What about Bill? Joe can hardly fall out with his half-brother.'

'Do you know nothing about families? No, I won't ask Bill.' I heard a muffled conversation, and then a change in background noise that told me the phone had been put on speaker. It was Bill's voice I heard next.

'You have to tell Joe if it's important. He'll probably be annoyed either way, but he's not going to fall out with you. He likes coming to the café too much.'

'Oh, so it's nothing to do with losing my friendship, it's just the free coffee and cake I give him.'

'Pretty much.' There was laughter in Bill's voice. I harrumphed as dramatically as I could and I heard Mark make an amused huffing sound.

'What are you two up to?' I asked for the want of anything else to say, aware that Pumpkin was still ignoring my presence.

'We are enjoying an evening of TV and wine, just the two of us, no one else, not a single other person.'

'Okay. Are you alright, Bill?' He'd answered my question in a sing-song lilt. 'You've not hit your head too, have you?'

'I am very okay, thank you. We have...'

'Ah, I take it Joyce isn't there.'

'Correct. She has given Florence Nightingale a run for her money and we will be erecting a statue in her honour, but I told her to bugger off.'

'No you didn't.' Mark was back. 'You didn't dare, and she has been wonderful, but we do need some time alone and I promised I would message her every now and then to let her know that I am okay. But yes, it was time for her to bugger off.'

'To give her her due,' Bill sounded deadly serious now, 'the woman has been remarkable. I mean, I always knew there was a pussycat underneath all of the leopard print and eyeshadow, but the love and care she's shown Mark... we're incredibly lucky to have her as a friend. Talk about a ferocious protector of those she loves.'

We fell into a reflective silence, until Mark broke it.

'Wait, wait, what did you say about Joe having plans in the marriage department?'

Uh-oh, wasn't that meant to be a secret?

36

*A*fter wrestling with my conscience all day Sunday, I called Joe as soon as I arrived at the office on Monday morning and was relieved when he didn't answer his phone. I left him a message about Kit Porter, and then pondered what to do next.

I was standing in the Library Café kitchen, staring out at the private lane that ran along the side of the building and was off limits to the public. A mug of coffee in one hand, I was trying to work out my next plan of action. I had a dead body, a series of thefts, a voodoo doll, a ransacked office, a keyed car, not to mention the attack on Mark. I wondered if I should pay more attention to Harriet, Sheridan's wife, or perhaps the case was linked to Sheridan's business dealings. Perhaps Elliot had been the intended victim.

'*Agghhhh*! What the...?'

A vision in multicoloured tartan and a mountain of vanilla filled the window, staring at me with a frightening intensity and mouthing something. I stepped back, spilt some coffee, and then took in the full view of Joyce, who had appeared without warning. I opened the window.

'Are you trying to give me a heart attack?'

'Biscuit fraud. I think that's at the heart of all of this. There must be all kinds of skulduggery – stealing recipes, sabotaging biscuit mix, ruining competitors' reputations. Sheridan must have got mixed up in some sort of sugary scandal and that's why he was killed.'

'Sugary scandal? Are you serious?'

'Very, we need to pay a visit to the factory.'

'For a start, Sheridan was no longer involved at the factory. He sold the business and only had an office there, which as far as I can tell, he rarely visited. Secondly, why would a biscuit competitor bother to kill him at the museum when they could have run him over or hired a hitman? Not that I imagine there's many of those in Derbyshire. And thirdly… well thirdly… sugary scandal? Get in here.'

Joyce's shoulders slumped and she walked off towards the door into the café.

Tina laughed. 'You can't fault her for being imaginative.'

'Have you been stood there the whole time?'

'Yes.'

'So I didn't just imagine sugary scandal?'

Tina laughed again.

'No, you did not. I will go and plate up a scandalously sugary cake for her.'

Joyce was sitting opposite me, tapping one of her talon-like fingernails on the table. Her tall mass of vanilla blonde hair had a thistle poking out of one side.

'Scotland really got under your skin, didn't it.'

'It is a rather majestic place.'

'Was it just Scotland that got under your skin? You never answered Mark's question about a laird in shining tartan.'

Her fingers stilled and she reached for her coffee. After taking a sip, she looked at me intently.

'He was rather majestic as well.'

'Who?' I squealed, and then checked myself. 'Tell me more about him.'

'First I want to hear about Ryan, I feel like I've been kept very much out of the loop. Are you serious about one another?'

'Serious? I haven't seen him for weeks.'

'I want another look at him.' Joyce scrolled through her phone. I could see that she was online and searching for a photo of Ryan. She found one.

'Tall, slim, smartly attired, wears a shirt, although he often lacks a tie, looks like he has a brain the size of a planet. He doesn't have a moustache of any kind, though, let alone one which requires sculpting.' She peered at me over the top of her phone.

'What are you on about?'

'You appear to have found a straight version of Mark, or at least I presume he's straight. If he's chasing you, it might not be advisable to put money on that, not these days.' If I'd been drinking coffee, I might have spat it out at that point.

'Are you saying I'm trying to date Mark?'

She handed me her phone and I scrolled through the photographs of Ryan. Bugger, she was right.

'I'm not saying there is anything wrong with that, although a psychiatrist would have a field day, but if you ever go on a double date with Mark and Bill, you might want to make sure you grab the bottom of the correct man when you return to the bar after you've powdered your nose. Perhaps you should give them name badges.'

I felt my heart sink a little. I loved Mark, but I certainly didn't want to date him, nor a heterosexual stand-in.

'Talking of Mark...' Joyce appeared to have moved on from that slightly icky subject matter with impressive ease, but then she wasn't the one who had started dating a carbon copy of her best friend.

'What about him?' I mumbled, still looking at the pictures of Ryan and really hoping he wasn't wearing a pocket watch in any of them. There were certainly far too many waistcoats for comfort.

'He appears to be doing remarkably well, under the circumstances, and I feel that I can start to reduce the time I spend with him. He has become rather dependent on me.' She tilted her head; the thistle looked a little precarious. 'What, are you chewing on a bee? What's going on?'

'Trying not to sneeze,' I lied, desperately fighting to contain my laughter as I recalled Mark and Bill's words from Saturday night. She didn't look convinced.

'Well, I have the afternoon off, so where are we going first?'

My mobile phone started to ring and Joe's name appeared on the screen. I took a deep breath.

'Joe, hi.'

'No, we didn't look for a Christopher Porter. We'll do a background check on him now.' He didn't sound too pleased. 'We'll have to bring him in if what you've been told is true. This doesn't mean you're off the hook, you know.'

'I didn't know I was on one.'

He hung up. Kit, or Christopher, appeared to have jumped a few places up the list of suspects.

37

Joyce had made the decision that our first stop was to be, in my case, a return visit to the Tasker biscuit factory. I hadn't been able to find out why Libby left the exhibition launch at what seemed like an inappropriate time and Joyce reckoned that was the key to the whole affair. I had agreed to return and talk to Libby partly because I wanted to see what would happen when the two women came head to head – the resulting fireworks could actually cause the space-time continuum to turn in on itself, and Earth and all surrounding planets would vanish into a great big black hole. Or something like that; I don't watch much science fiction.

Joyce insisted on driving us over in her BMW convertible. It wasn't warm enough to put the roof down, but the car still added a touch of glamour, and if it made us look wealthy and important, there might be a greater chance that we could gain entry to the building without an invitation. Not that I'd needed one before, but Libby might have had words with security about that.

Today's guard at the visitor's entrance looked like a giant tomato that had been squeezed into a uniform – red faced, very round and with oddly smooth skin. I wondered if he was going to explode before the planet had a chance to.

'Do you have an appointment?'

'No, Libby told us to announce ourselves when we arrived. It's rather an important visit and we just had to get here as soon as we could.' I smiled at him.

'So important that she decided to go out and get lunch when she was expecting you here any minute?' There was definite scepticism in his voice.

Joyce stepped forward. I expected her to flutter her eyelashes and try the seduction route, but she took a different path. Her voice became efficient and businesslike rather than 'lock up your husbands and sons'.

'I do understand your predicament, young man, and quite frankly, I think it shows your dedication to the job, but we are here on a rather urgent matter and I think that Libby heading out to get some sustenance was a wise decision. As I'm sure you are aware, the man she worked with for many years recently died in extremely tragic circumstances, and along with the matter we wish to discuss with her, that is going to lead to a very challenging time for her. Ensuring she has the strength and is fit and able to deal with the months ahead is, I feel, a very sensible approach. I am sure you wouldn't want to have to coordinate the arrival of an ambulance should she find it all a bit much and the stress of our meeting were to cause her to faint after skipping lunch? We all have a duty of care to our colleagues, don't we?'

The security tomato looked as though he'd lost track of her monologue about halfway through, but he also didn't appear to like the idea of coordinating the arrival of the emergency services. Wordlessly, he slid the signing-in books towards us, and then held the gate open. He didn't even bother to ask if we knew where we were going. I assumed that having pushed back once, he felt his job was done.

We half ran, half walked down the corridors. I took the occasional wrong turn, but knew I was heading in roughly the right direction.

'We have however long it takes her to buy a sandwich or whatever she likes to eat. How long does that give us?' Joyce gave me a searching look. I shrugged my shoulders.

'I haven't a clue, I don't know where she's gone. For all I know, she's having a seventeen-course tasting menu, each course paired with the finest wine, or she could be troughing down a burger. Alternatively, there might be a butty van in the car park and we have about three minutes.'

That gave Joyce pause for thought and she picked up her pace.

'This way.' I ran down a familiar corridor and stopped in front of the door to Libby's office. It was locked. 'You got a hairpin we can use?'

Joyce looked shocked. 'Do you really think I'm going to risk all the hard work I put into my...'

'Not even for Mark's sake?'

'Oh, alright.' She huffed as she carefully removed a pin from her cloud of hair and fiddled with it in the lock of the door. Nothing happened. She looked at me.

'Do you know how to do this?'

'Me? No, I thought you knew how to do it.'

'What do you think of me? Don't answer that, but criminal mastermind shouldn't be on the list. Oh, bugger this.' She stood side on to the door, swung her hip away, then back with great force. The door sprang open, leaving minimal damage to the lock. It wasn't immediately obvious, unless – like I was – you were looking for signs of a break-in. 'A bit of cushioning comes in handy from time to time.' She grinned, then her face fell and she rubbed her hip. 'I'm going to have one hell of a bruise. Come on, we don't know how long we've got and it's going to be a lot harder to come up with an excuse for being in here with a broken door.'

Pushing the door shut, Joyce immediately started opening drawers and going through them at speed.

'Careful,' I advised.

'That ship has sailed, my dear, I've just broken in, which makes me a criminal mastermind after all. There's no point holding back now.'

'You do realise we could end up in a police cell,' I said as I searched along bookcases.

'Joe will make sure that doesn't happen.'

'He will not, he's hoping to get promoted to sergeant. Not that he'd break the law to help us anyway. He will do his job and be heartbroken at the same time. He'll have no choice with our fingerprints all over this room.'

I turned to see her holding her hands up. She was wearing a pair of white latex gloves.

'Do you always carry those around with you?'

'You never know when they might come in handy.'

'I don't think I want to know.'

'Mark!' she replied, turning his name into an instruction. 'Come on, get on with it.'

'But what about my fingerprints?'

'You came here to talk to Libby a couple of days ago, perfect excuse.' She was right. I looked in the bin under the desk, I riffled through the filing cabinet, I searched a pile of files on the windowsill, but nothing stood out.

'We could have just asked her why she left early.'

'I thought you had.'

'She was scary, so I didn't pursue it.'

Joyce rolled her eyes and kept going. She reached for a bag that was hanging on a coat rack in the corner of the room and put it on the desk, rooting through it.

'You know what that means?' I nodded at the bag.

'She has expensive taste? This is Italian leather, unusual. I've not seen anything like it before, but worth a fortune, I bet.'

'No. It means that she won't be long. If she's not taken her bag and only taken her purse to get lunch, she must have just gone round the corner. Maybe there was a butty van in the car park after all and we didn't see it.'

Joyce was still examining the bag. Then she pulled her phone out and snapped a picture of it. 'The stitching is a bit worse for wear. Fascinating, though, I'd love to find out more.' Joyce's interest in fashion and design had a historical bent and she was a sponge for related information. She was like Mark in that way.

'Joyce!'

'Alright, alright.' She pulled out tissues from the bag, a number of nail files, a hairbrush, car keys – further evidence Libby hadn't gone far – files that matched those in the cabinet I had just searched, some scrunched-up paper, an empty envelope, a supermarket receipt, a newspaper clipping.

'Hand me that.' Joyce went to pass me the receipt. 'Not that, I don't care what brand of toilet paper she uses. The newspaper clipping.' I smoothed it out on the desk. It was an old article, printed off a computer, so it was probably something Libby had found online. I started to read, but heard footsteps down the corridor. Joyce's face froze.

'Under the desk,' she commanded.

'Don't be ridiculous, we'll have to...'

The footsteps passed by the office door and kept going.

'Let's go, now.' Joyce slammed shut the drawer she had been going through, took one more look at the bag, and then joined me at the door.

I opened it slowly and peered out. 'Now!' Then I led the haphazard run-walk down the corridor. What had my life become?

38

We were sitting in Mark and Bill's garden. Joyce and I had taken the executive decision to abuse our management positions and not return to work. Mark was working from home, but didn't appear to mind being disturbed.

The modern wooden garden furniture was made more comfortable with minimalist grey cushions, but it was set against a backdrop of vibrant colours. I was admiring them as Mark poured us all drinks.

'They're beautiful.'

'It's all Bill's work. He says there is something cathartic about having your hands in soil, while I'd rather have a mud pack and soft music.' There were broccoli-like clusters of little dark-pink flowers, star-shaped red flowers, light purple ones, spiky orange cone shapes.

'Ooh, I know that one.' Almost jumping up and down in my seat with the sheer pleasure of finding a plant I recognised as I was hardly known for my horticultural prowess, I said, 'That's a fuchsia. I love them, the way they hang with those gorgeous purple bells.'

'Well done, you'll be giving Alan Titchmarsh a run for his

money with your extensive knowledge. You'll love this one.' Mark pointed at a huge daisy with a dark mahogany centre and amber-yellow petals. 'That's known as a *cappuccino*. I only remember that because it made me think of you.'

After he had settled in his own seat, he looked at Joyce, and then to me with a serious expression.

'Your fingerprints will be all over that office now.'

'Mine won't,' declared Joyce triumphantly, pulling the latex gloves out of her bag. Mark screwed up his eyes.

'Please don't tell me why you carry those, I beg of you.' Joyce gave him a look which would have normally been accompanied by a cutting remark, but it never came.

'And this one has an excuse from her previous visit, so we're in the clear,' she said instead, jerking a thumb in my direction.

'I wouldn't go that far. The security tomato will remember us as visiting around the time of the break-in.'

'Security *tomato*? And I thought the security at the museum was less than perfect.' Mark picked up the piece of paper that Joyce had placed on the table. 'So, the newspaper printout tells us that Libby knows about Kit's little dalliance with the police. What's the link between Libby and Kit? Why does she have that article and what's it got to do with Sheridan's death?'

'Libby could be meaning to blackmail Kit with it, but I don't know why she'd bother and I don't know what that has to do with Sheridan being killed. What is she so afraid of?' I asked no one in particular.

'Perhaps Sheridan was the one trying to blackmail Kit and she came across the article amongst his things,' said Mark.

'Why? Sheridan was loaded, Kit works in a museum. It would be more likely to be the other way around.'

'Which brings us back to Libby.'

We sat in a comfortable, thoughtful silence. I was the one to break it.

'I'm going to talk to Kit.'

'Why?' asked Joyce. 'What are you going to learn that the police haven't got out of him now you've put them onto him?'

'Because you know as well as I that people are more inclined to open up to someone who isn't an official. If he's been nervously waiting for the police to talk to him, then he might have prepared what he was going to say and created an alibi. Alternatively, if he was taken by surprise, he might have clammed up. Either way, after a little time has gone by, he might be grateful for someone else to talk to.'

'A little time? A matter of hours. He might even still be at the station,' Mark reminded me.

'Then once he gets out, he might be very keen to talk it through, a way of coping with the shock.'

Mark slowly shook his head. 'What if I said you shouldn't be doing this? That Joe is right? I've already got a whacking great bump on the head, which could have been a heck of a lot worse. I don't want the same to happen to you.' He looked genuinely concerned.

'You've always enjoyed digging around with me.'

'Maybe I'm getting sensible in my old age.'

'Oh, how dull,' said Joyce teasingly. 'Well, not to fear, we will only talk to people together, side by side, the dynamic duo. Sophie will be the Lacey to my Cagney.' I noted that she had given herself the glamorous role, but chose not to remind her that Cagney was an alcoholic. It was Lacey who was actually the steady one, despite the chaotic family life, and was with the man of her dreams.

'I'll accept those conditions. Now bugger off, the pair of you. I have to be ready to film next week and I've barely started on my script.'

'So soon? But surely you need more time to recover?' Joyce looked as concerned as she sounded.

'I'm fine, I'm showing no lingering aftereffects, no signs of concussion, so I mean it. Bugger off, both of you.'

39

We found Kit in the museum's small library, which was off limits to the public. It smelt of mothballs and stale sandwiches. He was hidden away in a far corner, which had made him harder to find, but also meant that there was nowhere for him to run. He turned as we approached and then stood over him. Concern flickered across his face.

'Kit, we wanted a quick word. We won't take up too much of your time, we know your work is important.'

He didn't have a chance to reply to me before Joyce sat down and smiled. She offered her hand.

'Joyce, it's a pleasure to meet you.' He took her hand, but his expression remained stony. Clearly, he was not to be won over by her charms. He turned to me.

'Sophie, isn't it? What do you want?'

I pulled up a chair and wedged myself in between them, partly to protect Kit from Joyce if there was any suggestion that he had attacked Mark.

'We've heard that a voodoo doll was delivered to Elliot some time ago and we've been led to believe that you might know something about it.'

His eyes bulged. 'How dare you suggest that I would...'

'We're also aware of a little altercation you had with the police in the past, Christopher.' I tried to keep my voice calm and warm, the smile still on my face.

'How do you know about...'

'News travels eventually, Kit, it's very difficult to keep anything quiet these days. Now look, we all make mistakes, and I'm not saying that I think you're involved in these latest events at the museum, but... well, you can imagine how it looks, and Mark is a very good friend of ours.'

'*Very* good,' Joyce reiterated. 'Family.'

Kit put his head in his hands. He didn't look anything like the defiant busybody I'd met in the pub and seen around the museum.

'I've just gone through all this with the police. Can't you leave me alone?'

'We'll leave you alone when you tell us what happened.' So, Joyce was going for bad cop, which meant I had to maintain the good cop.

'Kit, we just want to know anything that might help us work out what happened to our friend. We'll listen, we won't jump to conclusions.'

He looked at Joyce, whose expression told him she'd already taken that giant leap. I knocked her knee with mine and hoped she'd get the hint.

'I'm not involved in any of it, I swear.' He sounded tired. 'It all happened a long time ago, when I was a stupid young man. My... um, crime was way before I started working here. My parents insisted I move back in with them after it all happened, and then I got this job. I've changed.'

'What about more recent events? Kit, be honest with me; did you send a voodoo doll to Elliot?'

His head snapped back up and he looked me in the eye.

'Who told you that? Who was it? I want to know.'

'It doesn't matter. Was it you who sent it?'

'No, no, I didn't. I heard the rumours that it was me. But I swear, it wasn't.' It seemed like the police had put him through the wringer this morning, he didn't have much fight left in him.

'What about other things? The damage to Elliot's car, the office break-in? Maybe the stolen coins?'

He looked horrified. 'I didn't do it, none of it.' His temper had risen again, just slightly. I gave him a minute to calm down, and maybe make some follow-up comments that might drop him in it, but nothing was forthcoming.

'Tell me about Libby,' I said. He looked confused.

'What do you mean?'

'Libby, Ian's wife. Has she spoken to you recently?'

'Why would she?'

'You're not answering the question,' said Joyce with a stern tone.

'I don't know what the question is. Tell you about Libby? What do you mean? What do you want to know?'

I pulled out the printout we had found in her bag back at the factory. It was now flattened and folded neatly, but still heavily crumpled.

'Why would Libby have a copy of this?' He sighed again, but this time it sounded more like resignation. 'Was she trying to blackmail you?'

He breathed deeply and, after a pause, answered. 'She said it wasn't blackmail, that she was just making a suggestion.'

'And if you didn't follow her suggestion, she would tell people about this? Sounds like blackmail to me.' He shrugged. 'What did she want you to keep secret?'

He sat back in his chair. 'The night of the reception, the one that actually happened, Elliot's office was ransacked.'

'We know. Sophie just mentioned it to you.'

He looked at Joyce. 'It wasn't me. I saw Libby coming out of Elliot's office. I don't know for sure that she was the one who did the damage, but I saw her coming out of there. The next morning, she comes into the museum, says she's dropping something off for Ian, but she takes me aside and shows me the article. She must have spent all night online trying to find something on me, and she struck gold. Made it clear that she would make it more widely known unless I kept quiet about seeing her. Said she didn't ransack the office and that it was fine when she left it, but of course, there was a chance no one would believe her.'

'Did she tell you what she was doing in there?'

He shook his head. 'No, I was hardly in a position to ask.'

Joyce looked at me and I nodded. 'Thank you, Kit, we appreciate you being honest with us.'

'So, you believe me? Do you believe that I didn't do those things?'

'I believe you,' I replied, and I did.

'We need to talk to Libby.' Joyce was pulling out of the museum car park as she spoke. 'We daren't go back to the factory ever again, so we can't see her there.'

'I don't know where she lives, that might take a bit of work to find out.'

'I'll have to leave that to you. I want to check on Mark. It's far too soon for him to be thinking about filming, he shouldn't be doing any work at all. He's pushing himself too hard.'

'He seems to be fine, Joyce. I think you can keep an eye on him from a distance. He has Bill and I have no doubt that if he feels unwell, he will stop and take a break. You know how often he appears in the café, he's not afraid of slotting breaks into his day.'

Joyce was silent, but I knew there was something she wanted to say. I didn't interrupt, but kept glancing her way. She wasn't typically shy about speaking her mind.

'He could have died, Sophie.' The words came out quickly, followed by silence. I decided to let her speak in her own time.

Eventually she continued, her eyes straight ahead on the road, her hands holding on tight to the wheel. 'We could have lost him. I don't know what I would have done if we had. I know I complain about him, but...' She paused, and although I couldn't be 100% sure, I could have sworn I saw her wipe away a tear.

'But he's still with us and he's fine. Give it a couple of weeks and he'll be driving you up the wall again.'

Joyce sniffed. 'Weeks? More like a couple of days.' She looked quickly in my direction and smiled.

40

Mark had suggested that I talk to Lord Eyre about the thefts, so Berwick Hall was where I headed off to as soon as I had finished breakfast and said goodbye to Pumpkin. She had taken up a vigil next to the radiator in the kitchen, which was where I assumed the mouse was currently holed up.

According to Mark, Lord Eyre had taken a great deal of interest in the missing collection items – after all, it had been his great-grandfather who had built the museum – and he took the thefts very personally. He had apparently been happy to talk to me when Mark had phoned and asked if he would see me. I had then phoned Tina and told her to call if there were any problems, which I knew there wouldn't be. I was spending so much time away from Charleton House that any feelings of guilt were starting to seem pointless because they didn't change things. Which, of course, made me feel even worse.

Over the years, I had made several visits to Berwick Hall, a medieval manor house which had been added to over the centuries and as a result was a fascinating architectural treasure, so I was familiar with the building and its history, although I had never stepped out of the public areas and seen the part that constituted the family home. It was Ananya who met me at the entrance and walked me past all the visitors who were showing their tickets to the volunteers at the gate.

'I saw him earlier this morning and he said you'd be coming over. I warn you, though, once he starts talking, you'll struggle to get him to stop. He trusts the museum staff to run the place, but he still views it as the family's private collection and is very protective of it.'

'So, why was Sheridan the chair of the trustees and not Lord Eyre?'

'He was, for a number of years, and then he and the countess decided to start a family and his time became limited. To be honest with you, I imagine he found it hard to be impartial when contentious issues came up. Ultimately, he felt the museum was in safe hands and stepped away. He's still very interested, though, and was extremely involved in the exhibition Mark and I put together. He had quite a lot to say about which objects went on display. It could get a bit tiresome, but I learnt how to manage upwards, shall we say.' She smiled conspiratorially.

'Any tips, then?'

'It will be a bit different with you, but I would say don't be afraid of interrupting him. He'll go off on tangents, but if you ask him a question, he'll grab hold of it and run with it, not even noticing that you interrupted. Typically, you will get the information you need out of him. It might just take a while.'

She had led me through to a courtyard that was off limits to visitors, past a sign that said *Beware of Dogs and Ghosts*, and deposited me at a door.

'Ring the bell, he'll be right down.'

The first part of the sign proved to be accurate as the eyes I saw upon the opening of the door belonged to a big yellow Labrador.

'Lily, wait, Lily. I am sorry, she's a friendly old girl and considers herself the welcoming party. Sophie, come in, come in. I've arranged for coffee, Mark said that's what you drink. Actually, he said that the coffee bean is your birth stone.'

I laughed. 'Thanks, Mark.'

'Is he wrong?'

'No, not at all, and it's just like him to tell you that.'

'How is he?' Lord Eyre asked as he showed me into a sitting room and indicated a rather tired-looking sofa with a big dip in the cushions, taking a seat on the sofa opposite. I lowered myself down carefully and was right to do so. My knees were almost around my chin, and as I'm five foot nothing, that's saying something.

'Well,' I replied, 'he seems to be recovering nicely. I think the exhibition has given him something to be distracted by, even though the museum is where he was attacked.'

'Yes, that was rather unfortunate, poor man. I like Mark, lots of energy, marvellous on television too. He was rather made for the camera.'

'Don't tell him that, or the camera will never be able to get his whole head in shot without filming from the next county.'

He responded with a roar of laughter. Lily just opened a single eye from her spot on the sofa next to him. The room was well used and as tired looking as the sofa, the visitors' money likely to be spent on fixing the roof or the variety of expensive problems that came with owning a building like this.

'Now then, I believe you would like to know about the thefts that have occurred.' He shook his head sadly. 'It's so distressing. I know there is a market for private collectors, or the thief might just be after a quick buck and it was either the museum or a store of some kind, and of course we don't have the security that many places have. How they'd know that, I don't know. Perhaps they cased the joint, as they say, or just took a chance. If they were on drugs, which wouldn't surprise me, then they might have been desperate and didn't make any kind of real assessment. I do wish we could find the objects, make sure the collection is whole again, but nothing has ever been retrieved.'

I was beginning to see what Ananya meant about his ability to talk.

'If I ever get my hands on them... Of course, there isn't any kind of pattern to the thefts. The objects are all very different, from swords to rare watches, a number of Flemish tapestries, illustrations torn from books, an awful lot of spoons. There was even a table – a small one, but still a significant piece. Everything taken was beautiful, some things financially valuable, some not so, but there isn't enough of a pattern to believe that they are being stolen to order, and the thieves have left no evidence at all, not a trace. It is impossible to know how they got in or out.'

'Could it have been an inside job?' I asked as he stopped to take breath. 'Surely not all of the collection is on display in the galleries?'

'You're quite right. In fact, only about 20% of the collection is on display at any one time. The rest is scattered about the rooms the public don't get to see. We have storage units that line the corridors, the basement holds a vast amount. That's one of the reasons for the extension we are building. We would like to have more on display for the public to enjoy, but we also need to expand and upgrade our storage facilities. Sadly, many of our objects are at risk of damage because of damp or moths, that sort of thing.

'We did wonder if it might be an inside job, but most of our staff are very long standing – part of the family, you might say. We monitored things, increased security for a while, but nothing would happen and everything returned to normal. Then we'd be hit again. We spoke to staff, gave them the opportunity to report any concerns anonymously. Of course, some accused us of not trusting them, of not believing them when they said that they had no idea.'

I guessed that Kit was one of the more vocal ones.

'Ah, Louise, thank you. This is my wife, Louise. This is Sophie, she works at Charleton House with Alexander.' It was strange to hear the Duke's first name used in this way; it made it sound as if we were office colleagues who caught up on gossip in the staff kitchen. The countess was a beautiful woman who I knew had been a model in her younger years. She carried in a tray with a cafetière and all the various accoutrements associated with coffee.

'Lovely to meet you, Sophie. You'll need the coffee, once he starts…' It seemed Lord Eyre's reputation was well known.

'How dare you!' He smiled at his wife. 'But yes, I can go on a bit.' He slowly pushed down the coffee press.

'Do you think Sheridan's death was related to the theft of the coins?'

'It's entirely possible. He did like to go for a wander in the galleries after meetings. There are one or two alarms that he could set off, but not many and he knew where they were. He enjoyed soaking up the history, as he put it. I think that having the galleries to himself from time to time was very much a perk of the chairman's position for him. There is every chance that he disturbed the thief, and knowing Shed, he would have stood his ground, attempted to protect the collection. If that's what occurred, then his heroic actions got him killed. He…'

I risked an interruption. 'But his body was put in the sarcophagus, which he loved. That seems rather personal and not the action of a desperate thief. Surely, they would have killed him and run, leaving his body where it was?'

'Ah yes, very good observation, and I did think about that, but the thief equally could have been looking for somewhere to hide the body in order to give themselves more time. There weren't many options – the cases are locked, the drawers that the public can open are too small and usually have a glass panel protecting the objects inside. The sarcophagus would have been ideal. After all, it was designed to hold a human body.'

'Talking of the sarcophagus, Sheridan said something about returning Masahanum to Egypt.'

Lord Eyre groaned a little. 'Yes, he had become more and more interested in the repatriation of certain objects. It's a hot topic at present and in some cases rightly so, but Masahanum wasn't going anywhere. He's part of an important collection, and let's face it, if we started doing that, the museum would be empty very quickly. We perform a great educational service and we are ensuring there is an understanding of the history of the world beyond our own borders. We're about to do an important study of Masahanum, so we are looking after him and the information we gather will be available to everyone.'

'Sheridan sounded very certain about his return.'

'Shed was very certain about a lot of things.' This was the first time I had detected a note of annoyance and I decided I had to tread carefully. I wasn't here to make enemies and Lord Eyre was friends with the Duke. Changing the subject seemed wise.

'May I ask about the curse?'

'Ah, the curse.' I could have sworn there was a little wink as the cloud of annoyance lifted. 'Utter tosh, of course, but a lot of fun to talk about at dinner parties.'

41

Mark was working in the back garden when I called round. I wasn't convinced it was warm enough for that, but he had a blanket across his lap and seemed happy enough.

'Is this a vision of the future?' I nodded at the blanket. 'Quiz show on the TV, teeth in a glass on the side, nurse bringing you a cup of Ovaltine?'

'If the nurse is a strapping young man, then it sounds perfect. No, I needed a change of scenery. Bill still isn't letting me off the leash, and I remain in trouble for going into work the other day, even with Nurse Ratched keeping an eye on me.'

'I can send him a photo, if you like, prove to him you're here.'

'It's alright, he's been phoning between classes and our phones have got that tracking thing. Of course, he's forgetting that I can leave the house without my phone. I'm not a teenager.'

'I don't think you need to be a teenager. There was a table of four women in the café the other day, all at least sixty if they were a day, and all glued to their phones.'

Mark grunted and I took it as general disappointment with the state of the world.

'You can have half of the blanket, if you like.' I shuffled up next to him and pulled the blanket over my legs.

'We need a fire and marshmallows on a stick.'

He looked at me quizzically. 'Why would we need a marshmallow on a stick?'

'Like the Americans, they make those s'more things.'

The quizzical look remained.

'No idea what you're talking about, but I'm guessing it contains the recommended calorific intake of the average male in each bite.' He was probably right. 'So, how did it go? Was Lord Eyre useful?'

'Very, and I'm not sure how I feel about saying this, but we might be able to add a name to the list of possible suspects.'

'Ooh, who's that?'

'Lord Eyre.'

'What! You have to be joking.'

'He seemed pretty angry about the idea of Masahanum being returned to Egypt. It was the only time I saw him lose his cool. It's basically a family museum. I know it was bequeathed to the nation, but Lord Eyre thinks of it as his own private collection, and Sheridan was talking about getting rid of a significant and well-known piece. Masahanum's sarcophagus appears on posters and gifts from the shop. Almost everyone who goes to the museum associates it with that piece, yet Sheridan was keen to return it to Egypt.

'You saw how set on that he was when he joined us in the basement. He'd made his mind up. He had money, no doubt a lot of contacts and probably a few journalists on speed dial. The minute it became public, Lord Eyre would have no choice but to agree to it. Lord Eyre's opinion, that the sarcophagus should remain here, isn't a popular one, not these days. His hand would have been forced and he would have had to agree that it was a good idea and he was all for it.'

Mark put his hands together and rested his chin on the top of his fingers. He appeared deep in thought, but it wasn't long until he spoke up.

'I hate to say it, but that's a pretty good reason to kill someone. I've always liked Lord Eyre, but these families can often cling on to their history like their lives depend on it. I was never aware of any animosity between the two of them, but then they wouldn't let it show, I suppose. They'd be all friendly on the surface, and then the lord would go and steam over a glass of port.'

'What about Elliot? Surely one or both of them would have discussed it with him, so maybe we should talk to him?'

Mark winced. 'I'm not sure we would be very successful digging around for information on someone Elliot needs to keep happy and onside.'

'Can Lord Eyre really make things difficult for him if the family doesn't actually own the collection anymore?'

'If I had to guess, I would say very difficult indeed.' He thought for a little longer. 'Did he say anything about the curse that was of interest? Like he can provide scientific evidence that Sheridan died as a direct result of the curse and we can forget about this whole thing?'

I had to laugh at that. 'He thinks it's all rubbish, but highly entertaining, and the tourists and schoolkids love it, so I think we can forget that angle.'

'Shame, it might have made life a bit easier.' He rubbed the back of his head and my heart rate immediately went up.

'Are you alright?'

'Fine, why? You look worried.'

'You were rubbing the back of your head, do you have a headache? Should I call Bill?'

'Not you as well, Sophie. I have a bad case of bedhead and my hair keeps sticking out funny. I've been trying to get it to lie right all day.' He gave me a little smile. 'So, while I sit here one step away from being pushed around in a Victorian bath chair, what's next for you?'

'We need to find out what Libby was up to in Elliot's office. She also has a part to play in all of this, I'm sure. Mind you, she's a bit scary.'

'Then take Joyce with you. It will be entertaining if nothing else.'

'Oh, don't worry, she agrees that we need to follow up on this lead.'

'Make sure you don't use the word *lead* in front of Joe. He'll be even more concerned about what you're getting up to if you start using the lingo, and once he makes sergeant, we'll really have to be on our best behaviour.'

42

I had made one too many appearances at the Tasker biscuit factory, so I decided that the best way to find out more about Libby and have the opportunity to talk to her was by following Ian home. Mark made a quick call to the museum security team, where he spoke to Ian himself. After making up a reason for his call, Mark added in a bit of general chit-chat, during the course of which he found out what time Ian's shift finished. Then all I had to do was sit outside the museum car park and wait until he appeared.

Quite what I was going to do when I got to their home, I had no idea, but Libby certainly had some questions to answer. As well as learning why she was sniffing around Elliot's office, I wondered if I might find out more about Sheridan and Lord Eyre, and just how far their differences went.

I decided that having Joyce join me on this particular escapade would not be the best idea. Pitching her against Libby might not result in the optimal outcome, and I really didn't need to upset the woman so much that she reported me to the police. I couldn't afford to annoy Joe any more than I already had. Besides which, Mark had made a very good point. If Joe became a sergeant, then he was making his way up the career ladder, and going for promotions probably wouldn't be helped by having a bunch of idiot friends sticking their noses in whenever a murder occurred. This wasn't a game, we'd learnt that when Mark had been attacked, but we also had Joe's career and reputation to think about. If I had any sense at all, I would stay out of it, pass on all my ideas to Joe, and then leave the case in his more-than-capable hands. But as Mark and Joyce would probably argue, and Pumpkin would insist was a well-proven fact, I didn't always have a great deal of sense.

Ian drove a small, slightly rusty and dented car. He clearly wasn't a petrol head, unless he had a garage full of shiny toys at home.

I followed him for about twenty minutes, trying not to lose him as I fiddled with my radio for something to listen to, but it was an easy route straight towards Matlock. Ian and Libby lived in the north of the town in a small semi-detached house. The sandstone coloured bricks and white and brown paintwork matched every other home in the cul-de-sac. Every garage door was painted brown and the driveways were long enough for two cars to park nose to tail next to a strip of grass. Most of the gardens were tidy, but no one had gone to the trouble of making them pretty, so the street looked well cared for, but very boring. From the little I knew of Ian and Libby, it seemed like the perfect fit for them.

I watched Ian turn into the driveway, then continued down the street, turned around and came back, parking far enough away that I wasn't obvious, but close enough that I could watch the house. I had no clue what I was watching for, it just seemed a good idea to wait for a little while before knocking on the door. I also wanted to be sure that Libby was home. For all I knew, her car could be in the garage.

As I waited, I tried to clarify what it was I wanted to find out.

Why had Libby been seen coming out of Elliot's office the same night that it was ransacked? Why had she blackmailed Kit with information about his past? What did she know about Sheridan's murder? I hadn't really thought about the possibility that Libby was the killer. It could have been that she had intended to kill Elliot and attacked Sheridan by mistake, but I couldn't believe that there were any circumstances in which she wouldn't recognise Sheridan. Had she and Sheridan had a falling out over something? Was she also against Masahanum being returned? But why would she care?

After about half an hour, I decided that I wasn't going to come up with any flashes of inspiration sitting in the car, and anyway, the curtains of the house I had parked outside of were starting to twitch, and the last thing I needed was for someone to call the police. As I reached for the door handle, a second car pulled up onto the drive and Libby got out. I quietly cheered, and then panicked a little. It was time.

My phone rang as I was preparing to get out of the car. It was Joyce.

'Libby,' she said with force.

'I'm watching her now. She's getting shopping out of the boot of her car.'

'Does she have that bag with her, the one we saw in her office?'

I leaned forward and squinted. 'Yes, she does, why?'

'I was rather curious about it, I hadn't seen anything like it before. Can't say I liked it very much, but I did want to know more, so I did a bit of research. Then I popped in to check on Mark, make sure he wasn't overdoing it, and that's where I am now.'

'And that's related to Libby's bag how? Does Mark want one? Is he convinced it will go with a pair of his socks?'

'I heard that,' said Mark. I sighed.

'Joyce, you could have told me I was on speakerphone.'

'You're not, I just have perfect hearing. Carry on, old girl.' That Joyce didn't respond to that retort told me she was still in nurse mode, even if she had been told to bugger off more than once.

'Mark and I put our heads together, and after disappearing down a few internet black holes, we think we know why that bag is so unusual.' I waited. 'It's about 200 years old.' I wasn't sure how to respond to that. 'It's a very rare 19th-century Italian leather and tortoiseshell handbag, and it went missing from the Pilston collection about a year ago.'

I sat back in the seat and watched Libby as she transported shopping bags into the house.

'Do you reckon you can talk your way in?' asked Joyce.

'I'll have a go.'

'Don't be ridiculous, Sophie,' this was from Mark, so it seemed I *had* been on speakerphone all along, 'you don't know what you're walking into. Let the police deal with it. If Ian and Libby stole other items, they have a lot to lose, and for all we know, they could have been responsible for Sheridan's death.'

'They steal dusty old objects, she'll be fine,' said Joyce. 'Besides which, if we get the police involved, they'll want to know how we knew about the bag, and our visit to the factory wasn't exactly… well, we weren't invited, let's put it that way.'

'You'll probably have to tell them anyway,' replied Mark.

'Sophie and I are not going to reveal our own nefarious activities if there isn't anything to be gained.' That seemed to end the matter.

Mark issued an instruction to me. 'Keep us connected and hide your phone in your pocket. If we hear you getting into any difficulty, we'll call the police.' Feeling emboldened by the presence of my friends in my pocket, I decided it was time to get out of the car.

I reached the end of the driveway just as Libby closed the boot of her car and turned back towards the front door.

'Oh, hello,' I said, trying to sound as surprised as possible. 'I've just been visiting someone up the road and I thought I saw you pulling in.'

Libby looked momentarily confused, and then appeared to place me.

'Yes, well, I live here.'

'Clearly.' I forced a little laughter into my voice. 'Nice neighbourhood.'

She didn't reply.

'I'm glad I saw you, I was hoping to have a quick word.' I paused, but no invitation was forthcoming as I made my way up the driveway. She remained where she was, stock still, so I edged my way closer as I spoke. 'I wanted to ask you about the night of the reception. You said you had something you needed to attend to and that was why you left during Elliot's speech.'

'Yes, that's right.' She glanced towards the door. It was open and I could see into the hallway, but I was too far away to make anything out.

'I was just curious, what were you doing in Elliot's office?'

That appeared to take her by surprise and she spluttered before answering.

'Why would I be in Elliot's office? I had to take a call, that's all. I was nowhere near his office.'

'That's not what Kit said.'

'Kit is not a man to be trusted,' she replied, making her way towards the front door and putting a foot up on the step. 'If you did a little research, you'd discover that he's not just an irritating member of staff, but that he is a criminal and you should not believe a word he says.'

'You're referring to his past conviction for stealing cars, and the unfortunate death of a pedestrian? Yes, I know all about that. I've spoken to Kit and I believe him when he says he saw you coming out of Elliot's office.'

'Then you're a fool.' By now, I was right behind her.

'Who is it?' called Ian, his footsteps coming down the darkened hall towards the door. If it hadn't been for Mark and Joyce in my pocket like a couple of Borrowers, I would have started to get nervous. There was nothing stopping Ian and Libby from dragging me into the house, and I'd never be seen again.

'Ian,' I called, 'great to see you.' I leaned around Libby and pushed the door open as far as I could before she grabbed it. Light shone from behind me down the hall and glinted off some kind of display on the walls. I had the time to work out what it was before Ian blocked my view – it was a display of rather old looking swords. I didn't know anything about the history of swords, but I could take a pretty good guess where these particular ones had come from.

43

'Sophie?' Ian looked genuinely surprised, and he was managing to sound friendly, even though I suspected it was an act. 'What can we do for you?' Even with his small build, he was able to fill the gap in the doorway, but it was too late.

'I came to have a chat with Libby, but now I'm here, I couldn't help but see a rather fabulous display of swords behind you. I've always been fascinated by the beautiful and intricate designs that were often engraved on them, could I come in and have a look?'

I made sure that I spoke loudly enough for Mark and Joyce to be able to hear, and I desperately hoped that Mark was on the phone to Joe right now.

'Oh, they're nothing special,' Ian replied with an awkward laugh. 'Just cheap souvenirs we've picked up on our travels.'

'You must do a lot of travelling.' It was a statement, not a question. 'Libby, you pick up some very interesting souvenirs yourself.'

'What are you talking about?' She was stony faced, but I could have sworn I saw sweat starting to appear on her upper lip.

'Your beautiful Italian handbag. Where were you when you bought that?'

'This is the most ridiculous conversation,' said Libby, stepping into the house and starting to push the door closed.

'Good to see you, Sophie,' called Ian as it slammed in my face.

'Did you get that?' I asked Mark and Joyce after pulling the phone out of my pocket.

'Every word,' Mark confirmed. 'We've already called Joe, and he and Harnby are on their way.'

'I better get out of here, then. I'll head back to yours.'

'Too late for that,' said Joyce. 'Mark neglected to keep you out of it, they know you're there, so you better stay put.'

'Thanks very much,' I groaned as I walked back to my car. I might as well make myself comfortable – the firing squad was on its way and I had nowhere to hide.

'Stay there and don't move.'

That was all Harnby said to me as she marched towards the front door of Ian and Libby's house. I had climbed out of my car and walked back over when I saw them pull up. Joe didn't say a word.

I watched as the two detectives, followed closely by a uniformed police officer, knocked on the door. After a brief chat, Ian opened the door fully and let them in, a resigned look on his face. The door closed behind them and I was left to stand and wait.

About ten minutes had passed and I was starting to get worried when I saw the curtains at the front of the house twitch, and then Joe appeared. He stared at me with a serious expression, before his face morphed into an enormous grin. He gave me a thumbs up, and then disappeared again. I breathed a huge sigh of relief and laughed out loud.

I could hear shouting from inside the house. True to character, Libby was not going to come easily. As more police officers arrived and the door to the house opened, I could hear what Libby was shouting.

'I didn't want any part in this, I told you… Look what you've done to me.' She didn't exactly sound desperate, more strident, and angry, and sort of 'told you so'. Not that I believed it. I was more inclined to think that she'd put her husband up to it, she had *I wear the trousers* written all over her.

As I listened to the strength and determination in her voice, I wondered if we had also found Sheridan's killer, that it had indeed been a disturbed robbery that just happened to be an inside job, and she had killed him. I was still thinking about that as I watched the couple being led out to two waiting police cars and driven off. I could see Joe moving about in the house through the window, but Harnby stepped out of the front door and made straight for me.

'Sophie, we need to talk.' I groaned inwardly, or I thought I had. 'What did you think, that I was just going to say thanks and let you drive off? Come on, let's go for a walk, towards your car. When I've finished with you, then you can leave.'

'How's Mark doing?'

'Good. He's not shown any signs of concussion and Nurse Ratched made sure he took it easy for the first few days.'

'Who? Oh, Joyce, right?'

I had to laugh. 'Got it in one.'

'I'd be too afraid to go against her orders too. Look, Mark got off incredibly lightly…'

'I know, we all do, it could have been a lot worse.'

'I don't want to have to give you an official warning, but…' She left it hanging in the air.

'Message received.'

'And probably ignored.'

We were both leaning against the bonnet of my car, watching

the comings and goings at the house as more people arrived. To remove the stolen goods, I assumed.

'Was there a lot in there?' I asked.

'Let's put it this way, I'm no expert, but I'm pretty sure that when we're finished, they'll be lucky if they have anything to sit on.'

I whistled. 'That much, huh?' Harnby nodded. 'Do you think they might have…'

'Killed Sheridan Tasker?' She peered at me out of the side of her eye, a look that I interpreted as *really? Are you still asking about the murder*? I wasn't sure how she could have expected anything else.

She shrugged. 'We couldn't find any evidence on or around the body to identify a possible suspect, and you know as well as I that there were multiple people in the building and the security in that place is lax at best, so it wouldn't have been hard for a non-staff member to get in and out, or even tuck themselves away during opening hours and reappear once the museum was closed. So, we'd need a confession, and one that sticks. She wouldn't confess to anything, even if there had been a crowd of witnesses to her crime, and him? I don't know, he doesn't seem the type, but it's possible. We'll have to see what we can get out of them during questioning.'

Silence hung over us again, until Harnby stood up.

'I ought to get back.'

'Hang on, how are you doing?' Despite her lectures, I liked Harnby, and I had been wondering about the situation with her uncle. 'Thinking of going for DI?'

'How do you know about that?'

'I think we've determined that I find out about most things eventually.'

Harnby laughed. 'Yes, I've applied. God only knows what people will say if they find out DI Flynn and I are related.'

'But you're good at your job. The gossip will settle down eventually, won't it?'

'I guess so.'

'If you want it, go for it, and to hell with the rest of them. Then Joe can step into your sergeant's shoes, get married and live happily ever after.'

'I beg your pardon?' She turned and looked at me. 'He's getting married? He's not…'

'I didn't say that. You didn't hear it from me. In fact, you didn't hear it from anyone, so you can't say a word. Promise?' She appeared to be giving it some thought. 'Promise?'

'Maybe, if you'll promise to leave the policing to us.'

I crossed my fingers, hoping she wouldn't notice. 'Promise.'

44

'I'm shocked, horrified. It's unbelievable to think he was stealing those items over so many years and we never noticed.' Elliot gave a slow shake of his head. 'I've been sat here thinking about it since the police told me, but I just can't fathom... how did it... it's incomprehensible.' He sounded genuinely amazed by the whole thing.

It was the day after Ian and Libby Wiggins' arrest, and Mark and I had gone to see Elliot once we'd heard that he'd been informed about the thefts and had sent a member of staff to join the police at the Wiggins' house. So far, the number of items they'd identified as coming from the Pilston Museum was already in the hundreds, and the count showed no signs of slowing down. The coins stolen from the museum the night of Sheridan's murder had already been confirmed as amongst them.

Harnby had told me that stolen artefacts had been found in every part of the Wiggins' home, which had been largely furnished and decorated with items from the museum. Rare watches nestled in the water cistern, objects lay beneath the insulation on the floor of the attic, inside the bag of the vacuum cleaner. It had been easy for Ian to take objects over the years –

he had access to every part of the museum, he knew which parts of the collection had lain undisturbed for years and no one would check on, at least not for a long time. Swords, sword guards, jewellery, pieces of embroidery, paintings, rugs, furniture, glassware – it had all made its way to their home, and his motive? He thought the items were beautiful and had become obsessed with them. Libby was just greedy. When I'd asked Harnby how Ian had managed to get some of the larger items out, she'd told me that he had simply carried them to his car and covered them with a blanket. He'd gone as far as concealing swords down his trouser legs when necessary. Libby had taken a huge risk using the leather bag for work, but we could only conclude that she never took it anywhere near the museum and that very few people elsewhere would be able to recognise it. They had been stealing from the museum over many years so her confidence had probably grown, and ultimately become her downfall.

'Do we know why Libby was in your office?' I asked Elliot.

'All I can think of is that Ian had told her about the safe. Occasionally, I put small objects in a safe in that cupboard over there if I've had them out for a valuation or a special request to examine them. It all depends on what they are. Perhaps she had hoped I hadn't locked it properly, or she thought she might be able to crack the code. Stupid woman. She might have thought the watches she ultimately got away with were in there, although she did eventually find them in a workshop.'

I looked over at the safe, which I could just see beyond the half-open cupboard door. The cupboard was large enough to walk into, and right in the centre was an old-fashioned black safe. It looked like something that belonged on display in the museum rather than being used for valuable objects. Mind you, it also looked incredibly robust.

The cupboard clearly doubled as a wardrobe for Elliot. A smart dark suit hung off a peg on one side, a couple of pairs of shoes had been untidily piled on the floor, and on top of the safe were what looked like a pair of brown trousers and a white shirt. Elliot was hardly a man interested in fashion.

We talked a little further about some of the objects that had been stolen. Elliot's relief at getting them back was palpable every time another item was mentioned.

'It will be a wonderful way to open the new building of the museum once all the work is done,' I said, imagining a special exhibition. 'Do you know when work will start on it?'

Elliot sat up a little straighter. 'It's not been decided! There's going to be a slight delay. We've decided to use this break in the proceedings to re-evaluate, ensure that the design is entirely fit for purpose, thoroughly review the security, learn from recent events. It's a vast sum of money to spend, and a huge amount of work to be carried out on a very special building, only to realise that we should have done a few things differently.'

It sounded logical.

'These things require a great deal of thought and we have been presented with a timely opportunity to examine our plans anew. Now, if you'll excuse me, I need to update the staff, and I believe the press office has set up a few interviews for me. It's a very good day.'

'You've heard the good news, then?' Mimi had taken our drinks orders and was frothing the milk for my latte, shouting over the sound of the steam.

'We have,' I replied. I didn't feel the need to point out that Mark and I had been involved in the stolen items' recovery. 'It's great news.'

'It is indeed. Free cupcakes for everyone to celebrate.' After handing over our coffee, she presented us with two cupcakes. One had the colours of a peacock feather swirled into a tie-dye effect, which was rather pretty, and the other had a little marzipan bee on it.

'You made these?'

'Of course. To be honest, I've not a lot else to do of an evening, and I love the smiles on the kiddies' faces when they see them, so I'm happy to do it.'

'You're going to have to give her a job, you know,' Mark told me as we sat down, taking our usual table in the far corner of the gravel-covered courtyard. The branches of nearby trees hung low and gave it a feeling of privacy, but still, Mark sat with his back to the rest of the tables. Press interest in his attack had waned, but it would return if Gary Endersley and his colleagues found out he had been in my pocket when I had spoken to Libby and Ian, and as much as he rather enjoyed the attention, he was still recovering from the attack and taking life a little more slowly and quietly.

'Don't worry, I'm already thinking about that. Perhaps when the café here closes for the winter, I can give her some temporary work. I shall ponder...' I took a large bite of the peacock cake and groaned. With my eyes closed, I enjoyed the delicate lavender flavour that was tucked away under the purples and blues. 'I don't know how she does it, the woman can perform magic,' I mumbled through a full mouth. 'What's yours like?'

Mark took a bite, taking half the bumble bee with it. He too closed his eyes.

'Lordy, if you don't give her a job, I will. She can be my private baker.'

'What is it?'

'Lemon, with the perfect amount of zesty tang. I'll have to get a couple more to take home, this is the stuff that foodie dreams are made of.'

When our plates were clean – because, quite frankly, not a single crumb was making it out alive – we finally gave our conversation with Elliot some thought.

'Delaying the building project seems to make sense,' I said, 'but is it really necessary?'

'I doubt it. Someone on the board must have got cold feet, or maybe Sheridan really was the driving force behind it and there had been doubts, spoken or unspoken, that could finally come to the fore. I don't know enough about the debates that went on before it was signed off and the funding found. But – and it might have been me reading too much into things – but did Elliot seem rather pleased that the whole thing has been paused?' He wrinkled his nose dramatically and folded his arms.

'I thought the same thing, but I put it down to the relief and excitement at the return of all the lost items.'

'No, it was different. A sort of relieved determination. Was Sheridan involved in any previous projects along these lines? We know he was on a number of boards and was meant to have been instrumental in the transformation of plenty of organisations. Maybe that's what we should be looking at – dodgy business deals, securing contracts for family members, that kind of thing. I think it's time to dive headfirst into the rabbit warren that is the internet.'

45

I had prepared snacks and a bottle of wine. I had also asked Pumpkin if she would promise to be nice to Mark. They didn't have the best of relationships, but she could either change the habit of a lifetime and be friendly, or she could give him space when he came over, it was up to her. When I'd finished explaining the situation, she gave me a sulky meow and strode off to continue her vigil next to the radiator in the kitchen. Either the mouse hadn't moved all day or it had decided that was a good place to return to after a failed attempt at escape.

Pumpkin largely ignored Mark when he arrived, which was perfectly acceptable.

'Is she in trouble?' he asked as she sat facing the radiator. 'She looks like you've put her in timeout.'

'She has a small furry friend who won't come out and play.'

'Wise friend.'

We settled down, Mark on the armchair and me spread out on the sofa. What we were looking for probably wouldn't take a whole evening to find, but there was no harm in making it enjoyable.

'Was it always cultural organisations he worked with?' I asked.

'As far as I know. There was an art gallery in Sheffield and I'm sure he said something about two other museums. Once he retired and sold the biscuit business, he had a lot of time on his hands and he didn't enjoy it.'

'Okay, so here's his biography on the Pilston website. It mentions that he had previously been on the board of two museums, an art gallery in Derby, not Sheffield, and a theatre over the last fifteen years, which meant he was doing some of this before he sold the business. He was busy.' I reached for a handful of crisps and continued to type with one hand. 'You check out the museums and I'll look at the gallery and theatre.' With that, we disappeared into the internet and the world of Sheridan Tasker.

A couple of hours later, Mark piped up.

'I've found something that might save us a lot of work.' He topped up his glass of wine, grabbing his computer before it slid off his knee in the process. 'It's an interview with him for an architectural website. Two of the other organisations he was involved with also had architectural projects. It seems he was viewed as a bit of an expert on this kind of thing, and the architects and project managers liked having someone who knew what they were talking about on the board of these organisations. The architectural designs of the museum and theatre in question were award winners. Perhaps that's why he ended up on the Pilston board. There were plans to renovate and they felt that he was a good person to guide them internally – a sort of connection between the museum and those involved in the design and build. Let's face it, I can't imagine Elliot knowing his metallic perforated exterior from his exoskeleton of vertical curved steel columns.'

'I doubt I would either.'

'Nor me, I'm reading that off a website. I see Elliot as more of a Victorian gothic let's-not-change-too-much kind of chap. He would have needed someone like Sheridan to hold his hand, which is an interesting image.' He looked at me and raised a single eyebrow.

'I must get you to teach me how to do that one day.'

'It takes years of practice, and a lot of vodka.' There was a scuffling from the kitchen and the sound of a rather large animal running back and forth. 'If I didn't know better, I'd say you had a Bernese Mountain Dog in there.'

'The dog would be more graceful. I guess the mouse is on the move. It seems to me that all the projects Sheridan was involved with were highly successful and brought a lot of publicity and acclaim to the organisations. Nothing dodgy there, so what about the angle that Elliot was the true target? He's had a lot of cruel acts aimed at him: the damage to his car, the voodoo doll, his office being ransacked, assuming that it wasn't the curse at work.'

Mark raised a single eyebrow again, and then looked back at his screen.

'I'll get the vodka, you are definitely teaching me how to do that.'

He didn't appear to have heard me this time. 'I should make a phone call.'

'To whom? The school of eyebrow raising? Are your teaching skills rusty?'

He ignored me. 'I'm sure I know someone who used to work at the art gallery in Derby, the one Sheridan was involved with. Casper, that's his name, we used to call him the friendly ghost. It was a bit cruel – the man was so pale, he was practically transparent. Haven't spoken to him for a couple of years, but I'm sure I have his number somewhere.' He reached for his phone.

'It's almost ten o'clock. A bit late to go calling people you haven't talked to in years, don't you think?'

'Hmm, true. I'll call him in the morning.' I let out a loud, exaggerated sigh. 'Is that a hint?' Mark asked.

'No, not at all. It all just feels very unsatisfactory. We have a small local museum that hasn't changed noticeably for over 100 years, then we have a flurry of unpleasant activity and a murder. You'd think that a place that has practically been preserved in aspic would be easier to read. The clues would all be there in the metaphorical dust, but there isn't anything. The person behind this knows how to avoid dust.'

'What are you on about?' Mark looked confused.

'Or is very comfortable with dust, or… oh, I don't know. I'd just like to wrap this up for Joe and Harnby.'

'And beat them to it again.' There were signs of a smirk developing on Mark's face.

'No!' I insisted. 'They both have a lot on their minds, I'm sure it would help if we could present them with the name of a killer. A sort of new job or promotion gift.'

'Let's go back to the day of the murder. What was different? Did something change? Tell me again what Sheridan's wife told you.'

'That nothing special happened. He played golf, a business associate came over, Sheridan was in a good mood.'

'And then at some point, he went to the museum. Who was the business associate? Do you know what he talked to Sheridan about?' Mark closed his laptop and put it in his bag.

'She said the associate had received bad news, but Sheridan was fine, so nothing had happened to him. He wasn't the one who got bad news.'

'All the same, I think we should talk to this person, find out what he told Sheridan.'

I heard heavy footsteps and a slightly odd muffled meow. Pumpkin was walking proudly across the room towards Mark, the mouse in her mouth. She sat in front of him and Mark grasped the arms of the chair.

'See, she hates me, I've always known it. She's showing me what will happen to me.'

I couldn't help but laugh out loud. 'You daft sod, she's

bringing you a gift. She likes you, or feels sorry for you. Probably the latter. Either way, you need to say thank you.'

46

'Thank you, Mrs Tasker, I'm very grateful... Yes, of course I will. If I hear anything at all, I'll call. Bye, now.'

I put the phone down and got ready to dial the number Sheridan's widow had given me. I had agreed to meet Mark at the museum later, once things had quietened down at work, but first, I had time to track down the man Sheridan had met with before he died while I took a quick coffee break in my office.

Dominic Harvey owned a factory that was something to do with plastics. When he picked up the phone, he sounded tired, but he was willing to talk.

'Shed was such a kind man. He was the first person I thought of when I hit a few problems, I knew he'd be happy to listen.'

'Did these problems involve Sheridan?' I was wary of asking him directly what had happened for fear he would close down, and then hang up on me, but instead I heard a long sigh.

'No, no, Shed wouldn't be so stupid.' Another sigh. 'Bottom line, my business is sunk. Thirty years hard work down the drain because I hired a criminal, not that I knew it at the time. I was a fool. Not that it matters. No, it didn't involve Shed, but when I told him my bad news, I also had to break it to him that I would have to pull out of sponsoring the museum renovation. I felt as bad about that as I did my business folding, it meant so much to Shed.'

'Was it a lot of money?' Being British, I was always shy of discussing money, so I didn't want to ask how much.

'Enough to stop the project going ahead. But even that didn't faze him, he said he would cover my donation, almost doubling his own original contribution. He also said that my name would remain as a sponsor. I argued about that with him, but he insisted. He said that I had donated the money in spirit.'

There was a silence while I thought about what Dominic had told me and how on earth it could have had any part to play in Sheridan's murder. The man had been even more generous than I'd thought, saving the museum project, and being a supportive friend. Sheridan did not deserve to die.

I thanked Dominic, feeling sorry for him as I hung up. He sounded so downcast. Hardly surprising when he had just lost not only his business, but also a very good friend.

I had agreed to help Mark pack up his things from the basement office at the museum. Now the exhibition was up and running, he wouldn't need to spend much time there and his hours at Charleton House were going to be getting back to their usual level, minus the days he was filming. Ananya had already been and gone, so it was just the detritus of Mark's mind that needed packing into boxes. Not that he favoured that description.

'Scattered evidence of my genius, if you don't mind.'

'Is there any system to this scattered genius?'

'Not at all, just chuck it in the nearest box.'

As we worked, I told him about my conversation with

Dominic Harvey. Neither of us could see any connection to Sheridan's death.

His phone rang. 'Hello, this is Mark...' He raised a finger in the air and went and sat in a chair in the corner. Convenient timing as it left me to keep working on packing up his stuff. The more that was put into the box, the more the room became a plain, slightly tatty-looking basement. There was no sign of the creativity and research that had taken place, there was no evidence of the beautiful objects that were telling a story up in the gallery. The room felt as it looked, desolate and empty.

'Thank you, Casper, I really appreciate that. The next time I'm in Derby, I'll give you a call, we must have a drink... Indeed... thanks again, bye.' Mark ended the call. 'That, my dear Sophie, was Casper the friendly ghost. His workplace had a rather large, rather expensive modern extension built about seven years ago, doubled the gallery space and started its journey into the upper echelons of the art world.' He didn't say anything else.

'Go on, then, was he useful?'

'Very, but I think it's time to say goodbye down here and sit in the fresh air up there.'

'And have a coffee?'

'And a piece of cake.'

Mimi was as efficient as ever and we were quickly back at our corner table. One or two leaves fell from the tree above as we sat down, and I was certain I detected a slight autumnal chill in the breeze. It was actually rather nice.

I stabbed my Victoria sponge with a fork and took a large bite. Mark didn't tease me on this occasion, he was too busy shovelling coffee and walnut cake into his mouth.

'I'm going to miss this,' he mumbled.

'That's right, you can't get a decent piece of cake at the place you work, the cafés there are second rate at best.' The wide-eyed, frozen look on his face told me he hadn't realised what he was saying.

'I just meant...'

'Don't bother, just tell me what Casper said.'

Mark put down his fork. It must be serious.

'Sheridan was on the board of Derby's Slater Art Gallery. Casper thinks that one of the reasons Sheridan was approached to join the board was because he had been involved with two other arts organisations that had recently been through a *transformation*, as Casper called it. Sheridan was deemed to have a lot of relevant experience, and let's face it, having him on the board, where he would be unpaid, was a lot cheaper than hiring consultants. There was some opposition to the amount of change that was being suggested...'

'Sounds familiar...'

'Indeed. Well, despite the opposition, eventually it was all signed and sealed, and the project went ahead. The museum was reopened and to great acclaim. However, in the following eighteen months, three members of the senior management team, including the director, left or retired, and the feeling was they didn't go willingly.'

'They were fired?'

'No, not fired, but pushed towards the exit.'

'Had they done something wrong?'

'Casper thinks not, not explicitly. It was part of a management overhaul so it wasn't just the building that was new and forward thinking. But the rumour was they had been the board members to oppose the proposals.'

'But Elliot is in favour of the change, he's been just as excited as Sheridan was. He seems to have been a driving force, so surely he didn't need to worry.'

'Ha! So you'd think, but it was all baloney.' Mimi was standing at the next table over with her hands full of dirty plates and mugs. 'Told everyone that, did a load of interviews, gave cracking speeches to help raise money for it, but he hated it really.

Thought it was a destruction of all that was special about the museum. Said the building was just as important a part of the collection as the artefacts themselves.'

'How do you know this?' I asked.

'He had too much sherry at a dinner one night. I had been helping out as serving staff, and we were both waiting in the car park for taxis home when he started off on one. Telling me he felt like the heart was being ripped out of the place, but that he had to keep his mouth shut, especially if he wanted to remain working here. The next day, he was a bit quiet when I saw him, but we didn't talk about it, and anyway, I knew he'd had too much to drink, and we all say things we shouldn't when we've had a drop taken. I wasn't going to say anything, either. None of my business, and I don't want to know about all that management stuff. Didn't when I was younger, definitely don't want to now. I'm happy just making coffee and cake.'

She walked away, and Mark and I stared at one another.

'Oh, I almost forgot, hang on, I'll be right back,' Mimi called, before putting the items she was carrying down on another table, then disappearing into the horsebox café.

'Here we are. I knew I'd kept it,' she said as she reappeared, what looked like packaging in her hand. 'It got thrown away, but I pulled it out of the bin and took it home in case it was useful in some way. I don't know what made me do it, but anyway, here it is.'

She handed us a tatty and torn box. The address label on it was made out to Elliot Knight.

'And this is...?' Mark looked up at her.

'The box that the voodoo doll arrived in. Reckon you'll know what to do with it, so I'll leave it in your capable hands.' She walked off as casually as someone who had just handed us a napkin or topped up our drinks. We stared at the box on the table, neither of us touching it.

'It might not help the police at all,' I said.

'I'll call Joe, tell him we have it, but not yet.'

'Why the delay?'

'Because first, I want to talk to the man who I believe nearly killed me, and I need a bit of time to be ready for that.'

47

We had waited until the museum was closed to the public. Mark didn't want to cause a lot of fuss, and anyway, we knew that Elliot wasn't going anywhere. I also knew that Mark needed time to take on board what we had learnt.

In the end, he was surprisingly calm, and as we stood outside of Elliot's office door you would have been forgiven for thinking that we were just making a social call.

'He can't do me any harm,' Mark said, looking at me, before knocking and walking in without waiting for a response.

'Mark! Sophie! Can I help?' Elliot looked surprised to see us, but no more so than anyone else would if we'd just walked into their office.

'Not really,' said Mark. He took a seat opposite Elliot and indicated for me to sit in the one next to him. There was silence as Mark and Elliot looked at one another, before Elliot broke it.

'Is everything alright, Mark?'

I don't know what I'd expected, but it wasn't this. Mark just sat there, staring across the desk at Elliot. It was some time before he spoke.

'I wanted to look at you properly, look at the man who nearly killed me. Who knocked me unconscious and left me to die.' Mark's voice was calm, but I could hear his curiosity. There was no anger or hatred, he really did want to understand.

'Mark, I don't know…'

Mark waved a hand in the air. 'Don't bother. Now I'm here and can look you in the eyes, I know for sure it was you. You didn't like us asking questions, did you. I'm just grateful I was the one you saw first and attacked, not Sophie. If you'd decided to warn us off by attacking her, then right now, I'd be leaning across this desk and I'd have my hands around your neck.'

I turned quickly to look at Mark; I had never heard him say anything like that before. He had a sharp tongue, but he was a gentle man.

Elliot sat perfectly still, looking to all intents and purposes like a bank manager listening to our arguments for being granted a loan. The two men had locked eyes and the silence was lingering longer than anyone could be expected to put up with, but I wasn't prepared to break it. This was Mark's moment.

It was Elliot who eventually brought the silence to a close.

'You are a man of learning, a student of history. You know that we don't simply learn from an object in a case, but from what surrounds it, the story around it, the wider context. This building is just as important as everything in it. It doesn't need changing or adding to. Some TLC perhaps, but anything more than that, and we would have been destroying an essential part of the Eyre family story, and the story of the objects they display here.'

'That was no reason to kill a man.'

Elliot seemed to baulk at that, and I thought for a brief moment that he was going to deny it.

'There was every reason. I am going to assume that you have taken the time to learn about Sheridan and what he has done for other organisations? He has decimated them, changed them beyond recognition and kicked out anyone who disagreed with him.'

'You know that isn't what happened.' It was time for me to speak up. 'All of those museums, the art gallery in Derby, they have gone on to receive great acclaim, and he didn't get rid of staff, he couldn't.'

'He made sure they wanted to go, he forced them out. He was an astute businessman.'

'He couldn't have forced you out, not unless he had something he could use against you.' I wondered if Sheridan did have something he could use against Elliot.

'Did he know about the voodoo doll? Did he know you sent that to yourself?'

What was Mark talking about? I saw him raise a finger on the hand resting on his knee and took that as a cue to let him run with it.

Elliot smiled. 'Sheridan found out about the doll from Kit, who had decided I wasn't taking its arrival seriously enough and brought it to his attention. Kit didn't care about me, he just liked to stick his oar in. It turned out that Sheridan had seen me in the post office the day I sent it. He must have put two and two together.'

'And the damage to your car? The ransacking of your office?' I asked. 'You were trying to make it look like you were the intended victim.'

'That's right, Sophie. I knew what I had to do, and if I could make it look like I had been the target all along, then it might make things a little easier for me.'

'You didn't need to kill him.' Mark sounded disgusted.

'It was necessary, to save the museum. That is why I did it. It wasn't personal, it was business. We both wanted what was best for the museum, we just didn't agree on what that was.'

'And once you were unable to influence him, you played along for the sake of your job, then you saw an opportunity to put an end to it all. You gave a very fine performance of someone who was as keen on the renovation as Sheridan.'

Mark was right, Elliot had convinced me that he was passionate about it.

Elliot looked smug. 'Who knew how much my am-dram days would have come in handy?'

I thought about my phone call with Dominic Harvey, of Harriet Tasker saying Sheridan had seemed fine after their meeting. An intelligent, shrewd man like Sheridan must have wondered about Elliot's true feelings towards the renovations, and here was a chance to test him.

'I guess the day Sheridan died, he told you first off that Dominic was having to pull out of the sponsorship deal. You must have been over the moon, the renovation couldn't go ahead without that money. More money might have been found, but not for a very long time, and while it was being raised, you would have the opportunity to formulate another plan, a way of stopping the project once and for all.

'But then Sheridan dropped his bombshell: he would cover the shortfall. You had been so close to achieving what you so badly wanted, you could almost touch it, and then your opportunity was snatched away by Sheridan's generosity. That kind of emotion is very difficult to conceal, both your delight at the project apparently being on hold and your utter dismay that it could go ahead after all. You had to stop him, make sure he couldn't keep the project alive, make sure he couldn't push you out of the museum you love so much. So, you killed him and got rid of the problem entirely.'

'I did, yes. I'm sorry that you had to become involved, Mark. I really didn't want to do you any harm, but you were both starting to ask questions, far too many questions, and you do have rather a reputation for working these things out. A better clear-up rate than the local constabulary, if the rumours are true. I had to make sure you were stopped.'

Mark stood up. 'Thank you for your time, Elliot. You might want to get on with whatever it was you were working on when we came in. I'll call the police after we've left and that should give you enough time to finish up.'

'No need to wait, Mark.' Elliot lifted his desk phone and placed it in front of my best friend. 'The project won't go ahead now, not for a very long time anyway, so my job is done.'

48

'I didn't tell you this, but Harnby is currently your biggest fan.' Joe took a seat at the kitchen table.

'I find that hard to believe.'

'It was announced this morning that she will be taking over as Detective Inspector. Sheridan's murder will be the last case she'll work on as a sergeant. It was a relatively high-profile one, and it was solved, thanks to you and Mark.'

'So now it's a good thing that we stuck our noses in?' I gave him a gentle nudge as I walked to the fridge to pull out a bottle of wine.

'I never said that and nor will she, but between you, me and the gatepost, she is rather pleased.'

'Did you find anything that backed up Elliot's story?'

'We did. There were paint flecks in the pocket of one of the pairs of trousers he had in his office, which matched the paint on the key and on his car. It seems he didn't think anyone would pay any attention to the clothes he kept in his office – they were right under our nose – and he used that to his advantage. There was also a shirt that had Sheridan's blood on it. We found that at his home, stuffed in the bottom of a drawer. It's harder to prove that he ransacked his own office, but he's admitting to everything anyway. We also tracked the parcel back and were able to see the CCTV footage from when Elliot posted the voodoo doll to himself.'

Something about that had been niggling at me ever since Mark had confronted Elliot.

'But he sent the voodoo doll a month ago,' I said, grasping the hitherto elusive thought. 'That would suggest he had been planning all of this, but how would he know that Dominic was going to pull his sponsorship?'

'He didn't. The doll was the first act in what was going to be a prolonged harassment campaign of people on the planning committee – including himself – to try and scare the others into pausing the project just long enough for him to find a way of getting it stopped completely. We found a couple of half-finished dolls at his house. It was all very creepy. After he killed Sheridan, he realised he needed to make himself look like the target and he ramped things up.'

'Well here's to confessions, and promotions.'

We clinked our wine glasses together in a toast. Joe screwed his nose up. I shook my head and sighed, but with a smile.

'There's beer in the fridge.' He put his glass down and fetched a can. 'And what about Ellie?'

'Joyce is taking me ring shopping on the weekend. You've not told anyone else, have you?'

'Not a soul.' Not explicitly, anyway.

'Thanks, Sophie, I appreciate it. And what about you, when will you see Ryan again?'

'He's invited me to join him in Oxford next month. Joining him for a few days of his book tour is the only way I'll be able to see him before he heads off to America.'

Joe gave me a playful look.

'A romantic weekend away, very nice.'

'We'll see.'

'What's this about a romantic weekend?' Mark burst in, followed closely by an apologetic-looking Bill. 'I want to hear all about it. Where are you staying? What are you going to do? No, I do not need to hear the sordid details.'

'Sorry,' said Bill. 'The front door wasn't locked, but I did try to get him to announce himself properly.'

'Sophie wouldn't have kept that information from me, would you? It wasn't going to be a secret, was it?' Mark gave his brother-in-law a pointed look, so I shoved Joe's unfinished glass of wine into his hand. Joe could share his news when he was good and ready, and hopefully after he'd had a positive response from Ellie. As for my plans, well, the cat was firmly out of the bag and I was unlikely to hear the end of it for some time.

'Ah, Lady Macbeth, you have deigned to join us.' Mark made a sweeping bow as Joyce entered, resembling an advertisement for the Scottish Highlands. She pulled the tartan stole from around her shoulders and tossed it at him.

'Find a home for that.'

I removed it from his head where it had landed. 'Wine in the fridge, snacks on the coffee table. Go on, make yourselves at home.'

My friends gradually wandered into the sitting room, chatting. By the time I followed them through, Mark was sitting in an armchair with Joyce looming over him.

'If you want this seat, you should say,' he told her. She remained where she was. 'Oh, alright, it's all yours.' Mark pulled himself up.

'You should know your place by now, young man.'

'It looks like things are back to normal?' I aimed the question at Bill.

'Very much so, but their love fest was starting to creep me out, so I can't say I'm sorry.'

'Well, the truth is now out,' said Joe. 'There can be no doubt that Joyce would go to the ends of the earth for our moustachioed friend.'

'Yes, and then push me off,' replied Mark.

'A correct assessment.' The look in Joyce's eyes didn't match the tone with which she spoke the words and I smiled, then changed the subject.

'Are you going to tell us about this majestic laird of yours or not?'

Joyce peered at me mysteriously.

'Perhaps after my next visit to the Highlands.'

'*Whaaat?*' My voice was higher pitched than I'd intended. 'When are you going? Is there really a handsome Scot waiting to take you salmon fishing and throw you around the room at an energetic ceilidh?'

'And show you what he wears under his kilt,' said Mark, to much laughter.

'You'll be laughing on the other side of your face when I'm Lady Brocklehurst and you have to take my hand and curtsey when you visit.'

'Is she serious?' Joe asked me quietly.

'I would have said no, but look at her face. She seems different.'

I had been worried about the thought of losing Mark if he left Charleton House to pursue a career in television, but perhaps it was Joyce who should be the object of my concern if the wistful look on her face was anything to go by. She would make a fabulous lady of a Highland estate, and I could imagine her modelling herself on our own Duchess of Ravensbury.

While Mark and Joyce bantered back and forth about how she would approach the role, I thought about how things had changed. There was a different atmosphere in the room. Joe would be pursuing a promotion and asking Ellie to marry him. Romance was in the air for Joyce. Mark's career was progressing nicely, and as for me? I wasn't sure. I was looking forward to seeing Ryan, but I had to confess that I didn't feel the level of excitement I would have expected. Perhaps he would sweep me off my feet to the backdrop of a beautiful city of spires and domes. Perhaps I'd find a fantastic coffee shop and that would be enough.

'Where's that ridiculous cat of yours?' Mark interrupted my thoughts.

'You mean my own graceful Bastet, my protector who is to be worshipped?'

'Yeah, that one,' he said, his words dripping with sarcasm. 'I have a gift for her.' Everyone in the room looked astonished. 'What? She brought me a gift the other day, I should return the favour.'

'Did she wrap this gift and add a bow?' asked Joyce.

'No, she carried it in her mouth and it had a tail, but it's the thought that counts.'

'You mean to say her gift to you was murder?'

'You're just jealous.' Mark waved a toy mouse in the air. 'Here, puss-puss.' Pumpkin, who had been watching all of this from just outside the door, strode in, looked briefly at Mark, grabbed the toy in her mouth and wandered back out. 'I will take that as a display of immense gratitude.'

'You really did get a huge bang on the head,' was Joyce's assessment of the situation. 'And if you ever say I'm your grandmother again, you'll get another one.'

Normality had officially returned.

Make sure you find out when the next Charleton House Mystery is released by signing up to Kate's newsletters at

www.katepadams.com

READ A FREE CHARLETON HOUSE MYSTERY

Building a relationship with my readers is one of the best things about writing. I occasionally send newsletters with details on new releases, special offers, interviews and articles relating to The Charleton House Mysteries.

Sign up to my mailing list and you'll also receive the very first Charleton House Mystery, *A Stately Murder*.

Head to my website for your free copy and find out what happens when Sophie stumbles across the victim of the first murder Charleton House has ever known.

www.katepadams.com

ABOUT THE AUTHOR

After 25 years working in some of England's finest buildings, Kate P. Adams has turned to murder.

Kate grew up in Derbyshire, the setting for the Charleton House Mysteries, and went on to work in theatres around the country, the Natural History Museum - London, the University of Oxford and Hampton Court Palace. Every day she explored darkened corridors and rooms full of history behind doors the public never get to enter. Kate spent years in these beautiful buildings listening to fantastic tales, wondering where the bodies were hidden, and hoping that she'd run into a ghost or two.

Kate has an unhealthy obsession with finding the perfect cup of coffee, enjoys a gin and tonic, and is managed by Pumpkin, a domineering tabby cat who is a little on the large side. Now that she lives in the USA, writing the Charleton House Mysteries allows Kate to go home to her beloved Derbyshire everyday, in her head at least.

www.katepadams.com

ACKNOWLEDGEMENTS

Many thanks to my advance readers; your support and feedback means a great deal to me.

I am extremely grateful to Rosanna Summers whose insightful comments made the book so much better that it would otherwise have been.

I'm extremely grateful to Richard Mason, my police advisor who guides me on procedure and makes sure I am, largely, within the law. When I break the rules, that's all me!

My talented editor Alison Jack, and Julia Gibbs, my eagle-eyed proofreader. It is always a pleasure to work with them.